# THE ADVENTURES OF DETECTIVE ROBERT BENSON

ANGELO THOMAS CRAPANZANO

ISBN: 978-1-957956-47-3 (sc)
ISBN: 978-1-957956-48-0 (e)

Rev. date: 09/20/2022

# DEDICATION

This book is dedicated to all the police forces that keep the people safe.

# ACKNOWLEDGEMENT

"I wish to thank Richard Stiff for all the wonderful revue and excellent editing he had for me on this novel and all that he has done for me on all the novels I have written."

# CONTENTS

# CHAPTER ONE

# THE RESCUE

**I**T WAS EARLY IN the morning when Officer Robert Bensen was driving down Embassy Parkway. He was returning from the University Hospital. He had to interview personnel there on the death of a nurse that worked there. It was a routine investigation to make sure they covered all bases. As he drove down the road he started to think about his future. He has been with the police department for twenty five years. The ruling is that when you reach twenty five years you are eligible to retire. He had originally planned to retire when he would reach this point and he and his wife Rita would travel around the world. Sadly Rita passed away two years ago. So he was wondering what would be the advantage of retiring now. What would he do? Both his kids were in college. The only thought that had come to his mind was to write detective novels. He had a lot of experience having investigated hundreds of cases. However, he realized that he enjoyed doing what he was doing. He loved helping people. It gave him the feeling that he was accomplishing something in life. He decided there and then that he would continue his job as a Police Officer. After all, he could retire any time after this year. He soon reached the street light at the east end of Embassy Parkway. After the street light turn green, he turned right on Cleveland Massillon road and started to drive south. When he was only a few feet from the bridge that was over the freeway, he noticed a car parked off the road just before the bridge. He realized that parking there was illegal. He pulled in behind it thinking that the driver must be in trouble. He got out and walked to the driver's side window. There was no one inside. He looked around and saw a person trying to climb up the bridge railing. Robert realizing that someone was trying to commit suicide ran up to the railing and fortunately he caught the person by the leg. He then reached out and grabbed the person's collar and pulled the person back onto the railing.

"Let me go," said the person. "I want to die" Robert was shocked to see that it was a young girl.

"You are too young to die," said Robert. "Why in the world would you want to kill yourself?"

"I have nothing to live for," said the girl, as Robert pullled her onto the bridge road.

"Tell me what your problem is," said Robert. "Perhaps I could help you."

"I have nothing to live for," said the girl with tears in her eyes. "I got kicked out of my apartment for lack of rent payment, so I have no place to live. I wanted to go to college but my bank tells me that my checking and savings are depleted, so I have no money. I no longer have funds there. I have no family. My parents were all killed in an auto accident. I was the only child. My best friend moved to California. My boyfriend just dumped me. So you see I have absolutely nothing."

"I think I can help you," said Robert. "First of all, I can provide you with a place to live. Both of my kids are in college and I have three empty bedrooms. So until we can clear your money problem you have a place to live. Now let's handle your money problem. Tell me how much of your money is missing and how did you get it?"

"Why are you doing this?" asked the young lady.

"First I am a Born Again Christian," said Robert. "That's what we do. We help other where we can. Secondly, it is my job. I am Detective Robert Bensen, a police officer. Thirdly I like you. You remind me of my daughter Liana. I am here to help you so tell me, what is your name and how much money are we talking about?"

"My name is Amelia Fredrick. I think I should have over $900,000 in my savings account. I don't know how it all disappeared."

"Wow we are not talking of pennies," said Robert. "Where did you get that much money?"

"First," started Amy, "my parents were killed in an auto accident. They had a life insurance that I received that was for $100,000. They also left me with a large house. I had no trouble selling it. I cleared $470,000 for it." While she was talking Robert was adding it up on his cell phone. "Next my parents had a bank account of $216,000," continued Amy, "which I had no problem, as the only relative to inherit it and transfer it to my account. Then I had $150, 000 in my account which I had set aside for my college education. That is about what I should have had in my account. When I checked with the bank they said that I had spent it all and that I had nothing left in my account."

"Did you try to find out what happened to your money?" asked Robert.

"When I contacted my parent's lawyer, he wanted a down payment, which I didn't have. He said it was going to be a big job."

"It looks like identity theft," said Robert. "We will have to take care of that first. As far as the other problems, you have a lot of time for a boyfriend. As far as friend and family you have me. I will act like your adopted father. As for friends I know my daughter and you will get along fine. So now before we attack your bank problems, let's get you settled in a place to live. Let's go to your car and get all your belongings. I take it you have all the important papers such as your birth certificate, your social security card, your driver's license, and anything will we need to verify that you are the real Amelia Fredrick."

"Yes, I have a brief case with all my identity information. I also have two suitcases of clothes. There is nothing left at the bungalow where I lived. By the way, please call me Amy. That's what my father called me."

"Amy it is," said Robert, "let's go and get you settled." That said they walked to Amy's car. "Will you follow me to my house," said Robert.

"I can't," said Amy. "I ran out of gas. That is why I stopped here." They removed the brief case and the two suitcases and place them in Robert's car. They lock Amy's car and Robert drove to his house. Amy was amazed and surprised at the beauty of the house.

"How can you as a police officer afford a beautiful house like this?" asked Amy.

"First of all I designed it and built it. When I built it many years ago houses were less expensive. Since I paid off the entire mortgage, I can afford to live here." Robert then took her all over the lower rooms. Next he took her up to the bed rooms. He showed her Liana's and Tommy's rooms first and then took her to the last room at the end of the hallway.

"This will be your living quarters as long as you want it," said Robert. "The rest of the house is open to you. Live here as my other daughter."

"I don't think I will ever leave here," said Amy showing Robert the first smile he had seen on her.

"You can stay here as long as you want, said Robert. "Right now however we have to go to your bank. You can unpack when we get back. Let's open your brief case and get all the information we need to establish your identity. Amy got all that Robert asked her to get and they left for the bank. At the bank a young lady approached them.

"How can I help you," she asked. Robert identified himself and asked to see the Branch Manager. The young lady led them to the last office in the room.

"Miss Fate," she said, "this is police officer Robert Benson and he would like to talk with you." She then left.

"Come on in and have a seat," said Miss Fate. "I am Karen Fate, Branch Manager. How can I help you?"

"This is Amelia Fredrick," started Robert. "She had over 900 thousand dollars in your bank and it seems that it has all disappeared. I am Lieutenant Robert Bensen a detective of the local police force and am investigating her problem."

"Well let me see what I could find out," said Karen and turned to her computer. After some reviewing she turned to them. "It seems like Miss Fredrick has written several large check to her Stock Broker."

"Why hasn't she been notified of this action," asked Robert. "We sent out a monthly statement to her on a regular basis," said Karen.

"Where have you sent these statements?" asked Robert. After a few minutes on her computer she gave them the address.

"That is not my address and has never been," broke in Amy. "I have not moved for more than five years." Karen went back on her computer.

"The records show that you summited a change of addrdess almost three years ago," said Karen.

"I think we are dealing with an identity theft," said Robert. "We will have to review all the documents that you have for these last three years and check the signatures for forgery. Also check for any pictures and finger prints on the documents."

"I will attempt to retrieve all the checks and have our own expert check all the signatures and fingerprints. Also I think I will turn this over to Lea. The computer information shows that Lea has handled all of Amelia's bank investtment" She then called Lea to her office. "Lea," she started as Lea waalked into her office, "you have handled all of Amelia Fredrick's' funds haven't you?"

"Yes,"said Lea, "the first time I saw her was about two years ago. She came in and had a change of address made. She then told me that she was going to write large checks to her Stock Broker. "In fact I just saw her about two weeks ago. She wanted to close her account which still had about twenty six dollars in it. What is the problem?"

"I have never met with you," said Amy. "I haven't been in this bank for over two years."

"And who are you?" asked Lea being confused with the whole meeting.

"This is Amelia Fredrick," said Karen, "don't you recognize her?" "She is not Amelia. I never saw her before," said Lea." She is a fake." As soon as Lea finished talking Amy pulled out all her records. She pushed them towards Karen.

"Lea, this is Lieutenant Robert Bensen. He is investigating this problem. I assumed that he had checked her identity. Any way here is her birth certificate, her Social Security card and her driver's license with her picture on it." Lea was so shocked that she sat down with a stunned look on her face.

"I think we are dealing with an identity theft," said Robert. "I think you have to dig up the information we talked about and get your expert to look at the signature and any finger prints you can find. We are going to the address you gave us and we will come bacck tomorrow to go over what we find."

"Before you go, just to be sure, please leave me a copy of your signature and your finger prints," said Karen. Amy did that on a sheet Karen gave her and they left.

On the way home Robert stopped at the Olive Garden restaurant. "It is almost one," said Robert. "I am hungry. I think we should have lunch before we go any fuurther."

"That's a good idea," said Amy. "I owe you so much I should pay for lunch, but I'm sorry, I don't haveany money." They both laughed at that statement.

"You can pay me by cooking a nice dinner tonight," said Robert. He was kidding her but she took it seriously.

"Will we get back in time?" said Amy. "Where are we going next?" "First, we are going home so that I can get a gas can. I think we had better get your car." Robert did just that. At home he got a small gas can and after getting gas he took Amy to her car. They put the gas in the car's tank and Amy followed Robert home. After that they went to the Olive Garden for lunch. Amy was again interested in their next move.

"What now," asked Amy? "Where do we go next?"

"It will not be necessary for you to come with me the rest of the day," said Robert. "I am going to the address we got from the bank.

I will have to get a court order from the judge to search the premises. I will also bring a couple of fellow police officers with me, in case we have to arrest them." After they ate, Robert took Amy to his house.

"How long are you going to be?" asked Amy wondering what she would do while he was gone.

"I really don't know" responded Robert, realizing what Amy was thinking. "Why don't you sit in the family room and relax. You can watch a TV movie if you like. Liana should be home from work about four thirty. Maybe you two can get to know each other and plan a dinner for us."

Robert then proceeded to get the judge's order. Afteer he got the order he went to the address with two other officers. The address was an apartment in a twelve unit apartment building. Robert searched for the landlord.

"Hi," said Robert. "Are you the landlady of these apartments?" "I'm Mrs. Mary Bradford, I own these apartments."

"Great," said Robert. "I am police Detective Robert Bensen. I am here to search the apartment of George Baden." Before she could ask Robert handed her the court order.

"Mr. Baden and his wife Martha live in apartment 103," said Mrs. Bradford. "However, I don't think they are home."

"That's fine," said Robert. "I can search for the evidence without a problem." Robert and the two police officers searched the apartment thoroughly.

"Hey Rob," said one of the officers," look at what I found in the bed room closet. It looks like a safety deposit box. The key is still in the key hole." Robert went into the bedroom and opened the box.

"Look what we have found," said Robert. "It looks like four check books to different banks and a driver's license with Martha's picture but Amy's name on it. I think this is all we will need." Just then the other officer walked in.

"Look what I found in the desk. It is a note with Amy's name and her social security number on it. I also found a packet of Amy's checks. I also found a travel sheet that say's they are on a trip to Los Vegas and will be back tomorrow at Akron Canton Airport at five in the afternoon"

"Great," said Robert. "You and Bill go there tomorrow and arrest them both. Now, let's go to the four banks that the four checks are from. We can see if we can freeze any deposits either one has there."

"Don't we need a court order?" said one of the officers.

"If so we will ask them to freeze all the funds until we get a court order. I just don't want to wait any longer." They then went to the nearest bank first.

"What can I do for you?" said a young lady as they walked in. "I am Detective Robert Bensen," said Robert. "I am here to find out what accounts George and Martha Baden have here and ask to freeze them."

"Follow me," said the young lady. She then let them into her office. What was that name again?" she asked as she sat by her computer. Robert gave her the name and she typed it into her computer. "The only accounts here are under George Baden. He has a checking account and a money market account. They both have been frozen."

"Can you tell me who request the account freeze," asked Robert. "We have a court order from a Judge Bradford," said the young lady.

"Thank you so much for your time." Said Robert and they got up and left. As they got into the car Bill turned to Robert.

"What do we do now?" he asked.

"I think we don't need to go to the other banks," said Robert. "I think I will just call them to make sure they all got the court order." After returning to the police station Robert called the other banks. They had the same message. Amy's bank had done their duty. As he was about to leave, he was told that the Captain wanted to see him.

"Hi, Robert," said Captain Wilson as Robert walked into his office. "Please sit for a while. I will only take two minutes of your time. I know that you want to retire. I understand that. You have been a valuable member of this team. However, I would like to make a suggestion. If you do decide to retire I would like you to be available as a part time member. You have a lot of experience and a very keen eye to get evidence in a criminal investigation. I don't have anyone else who could do your job."

"Sounds like something I could live with," said Robert. "Please retire me right now." After they filled out all the papers the captain turned to Robert.

"Good, with that done, I have a part time assignment for you. A young woman was found in the woods on Cleveland Massillon Road. She was unconscious. She was found by a couple of kids walking down the road. They called us. Our officers went and after seeing her, they called an ambulance. She was taken to Akron General Hosspital. I don't know if she survived or not. I was told that she was seriously hurt. I would like you to investigate this and find out what happened to her."

"I will go right after I have dinner," said Robert. Being excused by the captain he left for home.

When Robert got home he was surprised by a wonderful dinner that Amy and Liana had prepared. It was sausage casserole.

"It was fantastic," Robert told the girls. "You guys have out done yourselves.

The next morniing after breakfast, Robert told the girls that he had to go. "I have a new assignment. See you when I get back. I will tell you all about it if it's not too late."

"Get back early," said Amy. "We have a lot to talk about." "I'll try," said Robert and left.

Robert got to the hospital at about seven thirty. The nurse at the reception desk recognized Robert.

"Hi, Officer Bensen, how are you? It's good to see you. What can I do for you?"

"They brought in a woman who had been seriously hurt. Can you tell me if she is alright and where is she located?"

"She didn't look to good," said the nurse. "Her head was all bloody. She is in room 312." Robert thanked her and went to the third floor. There he met the attending nurse.

"Hi" said Robert. "I'm Detective Bensen. I would like to see the woman that was brought in this afternoon."

"She is in bad shape. The doctor is with her now. Go ahead and go to room 312." Robert went into the room. The doctor turned toward Robert.

"I'm Detective Bensen," said Robert introducing himself. "I'm here to investigate what happened to this poor woman."

"I'm Doctor Brenner. "I don't think you will be able to talk with her soon if at all. She had a severe blow on her head. Her lifef is hanging on a thread. It is 'touch and go' as the saying goes. I will hopefully know better tomorrow if she will survive."

"Well I'll be back tomorrow. I hope that she survives. We would like to know who did this to her."

"We would also," said the doctor as he left the room. Robert then turned around and left for home. Later that day, Robert cooked a salmon fish dinner for the girls. When the girls came home they were delighted to have dinner with Robert. Where have you girls been," asked Robert after they had eaten.

"Daddy," said Ammy, "Liana took me to show me the place where she works. She has a very nice job. It's the kind I would like after I graduate from college."

The next morning was Sunday. Robert got up early and took the girls to Church. After the service, Robert took Amy to the pastor's office. Liana waited out in the lobby.

"Amy," started Robert just before they went into the office, "I want you to talk to the pastor about your faith. I think you need some advice. Tell him your story."

"Whatever you say," said Amy with a questioning look on her face. She then was called into the office by the Church Secretary. Robert went and waited with Liana. About fifteen minutes later Amy came out with a big smile on her face. Before Robert could ask her any questions she yelled out.

"Daddy," she said, "I am a Born Again Christian. I have accepted Jesus Christ as my savior. Nothing on earth can hurt me now."

"Oh Amy sweetheart," said Robert. "I am so happy for you. Let's go home and celebrate." They did just that. Robert made Filet Minion steak for lunch. They had joy the rest of the day.

Monday morning after a simple breakfast, Robert left for the hospital. The girls had already left. Robert wondered where Amy went. He knew that Liana was at work. She worked at the University Hospital as an assistant at the University Lab. When Robert got to the hospital, he quickly went up to the third floor. He met the floor nurse.

"Has there been any change in the lady in room 312," asked Robert.

"Well she is still alive," said the nurse. "The doctor thought that she would not make it this morning. So I guess it is good news. Go right in" Robert went into room the girl was in. He walked up to her and looked at her face. Her face was still black and blue, but she still looked beautiful. Robert couldn't understand why looking at her brought such a feeling to his stomaach. He sat down and held her hand. That alone thrilled him. About an hour later the doctor walked in.

"I see that you are back," said the doctor. "I'm sorry but she is still unconscious. To tell you the truth I'm surprised that she is still alive. The swelling on her head is putting a lot of pressure on her brain. But it has come down a little since last night. Last night due to the pressure on her brain the rest of her body, especially her heart were being affected."

"How were they affected?" asked Robert.

"Well her heart for one was beating very irregularly. It was missing several beats and then recovering. At times her body would tremble and shake. Please go and wait in the waiting room and let me make a thorough exam on her." The doctor then had her brought down to the hospital lab. Robert thought that it would only take a short time before the doctor would have them bring her back up. But when it got to eleven thirty, he decided to go down stairs to the cafeteria and have lunch. He had a hamburger and a soda and went back up stairs. The girl was still not there. It was about three o'clock before she was brought back up. The doctor walked in behind her.

"Well," asked Robert. "What have you found out? Is she going to make it?"

"It looks good," said the doctor. "We made a very extensive series of test on her complete body. We evaluated the results and were very surprised and thrilled in what we found. Her heart and all her organs are back to normal operation. We could find nothing that wasn't back to normal. Our only concern now is how much damage was done to her brain. We will not know that until she wakes up."

"When do you think she will wake up?" asked Robert feeling a concern he didn't understand.

"I have no way of even guessing on that. It could be in a few hours from now or perhaps days. We will just have to wait and see."

"I will stay with her for a little while and keep watch over her," said Robert.

"As you wish," said the doctor. "If she does wake up, please have the nurse call me." With that saidthe doctor left. Robert grabbed her hand and held it tight as he reclined on the chair. What he  felt holding her hand was so relaxing that he fell asleep. When he woke up it was five o'clock. He then got up gave the girl a final firm squeezed to her hand and left.

When he got home the girls were cooking a dinner.

"I sorry I am so late," said Robert. "I was planning on making dinner. I'm so sorry girls."

"That is alright" said Liana. "Amy and I are having fun learning new dinner creations. Today we have a new dinner called Meatloaf. I hope you will like it"

"I'm sure I will," said Robert. "Maybe you girls will have to teach me how to cook" Liana served the meal. They all enjoyed it. When they had finished the meatloaf, Amy served a cupcake that she had made. They all enjoyed the cupcakes with coffee that the girls had prepared.

"By the way Amy," said Robert. "A couple of days ago you said that we needed to talk. I'm sorry that I forgot to bring it up sooner. What was that all about?"

"Oh it was no problem," said Amy. "I was just wondering if it was alright for me to go to the bank and ask how things were going. When I realized how busy you were, I decided to go myself. I went and found out that one bank had proceeded to returned my money. The other banks were waiting on the results of the trial.  Anyway there was enough money so that they gave me a new checking accoount and are sending me a new Visa credit card."

"I hope the other banks are not holding back on honoring the Judge's Court Order to freeze the accounts," said Robert.

"Was there anything else you wanted to talk about," asked Robert "Yes said Amy," You know everything about me and I know nothing about you." Just then the phone rang. Robert picked up and answered it. "Hi," said Robert. "What can I do for you?" "Is this Rob," said Captain Wilson.

"Yes this is me," said Robert, "What can I do for you?"

"If you have finished eating I would like you and Amy Fredrick to come to my office as soon as you can."

"We have finished eating," said Robert. "We will be right there." Then turning to Amy, Robert informed her. "The Captain would like to see us as soon as we can. I told him that we will be right there. So get your purse and let's go." They both got to the Captains office about ten minutes later.

"What's up?" Robert asked the Captain. The Captain ignoring Robert turned to Amy.

"You are Amy Fredrick is that correct?" he asked. "Yes, I'm Amelia Fredrick" responded Amy.

"I want you to meet someone," said the Captain. Then turning to the secretary he said, "Please have them bring in the prisoners." A few minutes later a police brought George and Martha into the Captain's room.

"George," yelled Amy, being surprised that they had already arrested him. "How can you do this to me? I loved you so much. If you had told me you had a problem, I would have given you some money. You only had to ask me."

"I was too embarrassed to ask you," responded George. "Originally I didn't intend to take all of your money. However, after some thought I decided that the hatred you would have for me would be the same if I took all that I could. I really didn't think that I could take it all. It was Martha that came up with the fantastic plan. We believed and were sure you would never find out what had happen to your money."

"Oh fine," said Martha, "put the entire blame on me."

"Come on Dad," said Amy to Robert. "Let's get out of here before I start hitting him."

"Isn't that unlawful," said George in his defense, "a police officer should not be assigned to defend his owndaughter."

"She is not my daughter," responded Robert. "She calls me that because she is grateful of all I have done for her." Then turning to the Captain, Robert asked "Is that all you needed? Can we leave now?"

"Yes," said the captain. "We have all we need." Robert and Amy left and went home. Liana was there and wanted to know every thing that went on. Amy filled her in with high emotion.

"He will get what he deserves," said Liana. "Just trust Dad." After a few cups of coffee they all went to bed.

The next morning Robert made breakfast for the girls, and afterwards went to the hospital to see how the young lady was doing. He wanted to know who she was and who struck her so he could punish him. Giving salutations to the nurse he walked in the hospital room. The woman was still unconscious. He sat down next to her and held her hand. Suddenly he felt like he was holding Rita's hand. Before he could react to the feeling the doctor walked into the room. Robert, without hesitation said,

"Hello Doc. How is she doing? Her face looks better."

"She is a little better," said the doctor. "I'm just worried about any damage to her brain. Everything else is back to normal. However, all indications are that she will be unconscious for a few more days. I know that you are busy so why don't you come back tomorrow late in the afternoon, or just call in. The nurse can tell you how close she is to waking up. I will keep her informed."

"Very well Doctor," said Robert. "I would like to close this case as soon as I can. We have found no evidence on who did this to her." Robert said this to ward off any idea that there was any other reason for him to be there.

When he got home he found that the girls were not home. He then went back to writing his book. About four thirty he made dinner so that when they go home they would have a nice dinner waiting for them. They both showed up about a quarter to five.

"Where have you girls been?" asked Robert.

"That is a very interesting question," said Amy. "At least the answer is. As you know that before we met I had taken the entrance exam at Cleveland State Nursing School and was accepted. Yesterday I went there and rented a place to stay when I'm in school. Today Liana got permission for me to work with her at the University hospital lab. It's a student position. There is no pay. I just assist patients."

"Wow, that is fantastic," said Robert. "But isn't it kind of early to rent a room?"

"I just wanted to be sure I had a place to stay. I heard that if you wait too long there will not be any place available. As long as I pay the rent they were happy. By the way, I heard from the bank. They said that I got most of my money back from the other banks. So I have plenty of money to pay for the rent."

"I'm so happy for you," said Robert. "Not only that, but now Liana has a friend to keep her company."

"I'm more than a friend," said Liana breaking into the conversation. "I am more like a sister. Remember that she calls you Dad, that action makes her my sister." Every one smiled. They all liked the thought.

"By the way Amy," said Robert turning to Amy. "You said something about my knowing all about you but you knew nothing about me. Is now a good time to talk about it?"

"I would like that very much," said Amy. "Liana has given me a little information about your family."

"Well there isn't that much to tell you," said Robert. "First I have a son who lives in Medina. He has purchased a home there. He did that because he opened an office there. He is an Optometrist. Next I have a sister that lives not too far from here. She lives on Elgin Street. She is a very busy woman. You will meet her on the fourth of July if not earlier. My parents live in Garfield Height. It is a city just on the southern end of Cleveland. My father's name is Thomas. That's why, according to customs, I name my son Thomas. My father was a worker at the US steel company. He is now retired. My mother's named is Liana as you can figure out. I will take you to meet them soon. She always comes here for Thanksgiving dinner. As for me, I think you know all about what I do. According to the law, I can't tell you about any of the cases I've worked on. Does thhat answer all of your questions?"

"Yes," said Amy. "Thank you very much. I can't wait to meet the rest of your family."

The next day, Robert went to the hospital to see if the woman had awakened. The nurse told him to go into the room because the doctor was there. He was the only one who would know.

"Hi doc," said Robert. "How is our patient doing? Is there any hope that she will awaken today?"

"I think the chances are less than one percent, "said the doctor. "The tests show that the brain activity, especially in that damaged area, is not functioning properly to put it bluntly. I think it will take about a week before it will be functioning well enough for her to come out of her comma. I will also give her medication to keep her sedated to keep her brain relaxed. Look, I know that you are very busy. Why don't you just call in every morning? I will keep the nurse informed of her condition. Whenever there is a chance of her waking we will let you know."

"Thanks Doctor," said Robert. "That would be a relief." He was lying. He was going to miss holding her hand.

The next week was a very boring week. The girls were never home. The Captain didn't have any assignment for him. All he could do is work on writing his novel. He called the hospital every day. It was about four days later that the nurse called.

"The doctor thinks that she is close to awakening," said the nurse. "He is with her now doing a test of her brain activity. I called him because I hear her moaning this morning."

"Thank you," said Robert. "I will be right ovver." Robert cleaned himself up dressed in a nice suit and left. When he got to the hospital he went right into the room. The doctor was still there.

"How is she doing?" asked Robert without even saying hello to the doctor or even the nurse when he passed herin the hall.

"She should wake up any time now," said the doctor. "I just

finished checking her and everything tells me that she should wake up any time now."

"I guess that I will just sit here and wait. I don't have any other thing to do at this time"

"As you wish," said the doctor and left. Robert sat next to the bed and held the woman's hand. He loved the feel of her skin. It was about an hour later that he felt her withdraw her hand. She moved around lightly on the bed and then went back to sleep. Things were very quiet except for the nurse coming in every once in a while to see if anything had changed. It was about eleven when she turned on her side and started to make sounds from her mouth. At first it sounded like a slight moaning sound but soon it sounded like the purring sound of a happy cat in an affectionate mood. He thought that he should call the nurse but then decided not to. He decided to turn her on her back as she had been before. The sound that she had made before was no longer there. She was back to the way she was earlier. At about twelve Robert decided to go down stairs to the cafeteria and have lunch. Since he was in a hurry he ordered a cheese burger and a cup of coffee. When he finish he went back upstairs. She was like he had left her. She did move a little and make some moaning sounds every once in a while.

"Come on lady," he said. "Wake up. What are you doing? Are you dreaming of the moment you were attacked." About three in the afternoon she turned again and made the sound like a cat. This time Robert let her stay that way. A few minutes later she returned to the way she was earlier. It was about four when the doctor walked into the room.

"Has she shown any signs of awakening?" asked the doctor. "She has made some difference." Robert then explained all the noises she had make and her turning on her side twice.

"How about waiting outside for a few minutes and let me check a few things," said the doctor. Robert did as the doctor asked. He however stayed just outside the door. About a couple of minutes later the doctor called him back in. "I just gave her a shot. She should wake up any minute now." As they were both standing in front of the bed, they heard her moaning. Soon she opened her eyes. She looked at Robert.

"Hi" she said with a smile on her face. Robert was shocked at her voice. "Hi" she said again sincehe didn't answer. "Do I know you?"

"Hi" Robert answered. "I'm Robert Bensen. I'm here to investigate what happened to you. First, what is your name?"

"My name?" she answered. "My name is... I don't know my name. Oh lord I don't know my name" She then looked like she was going into a wild frenzy.

"Don't worry," said the doctor. "That is perfectly normal for the type of injury you had. I'm Doctor Brenner. I will take care of you." At that she calmed down a bit.

"What happened to me?" she asked with a worried look on her face. How did I get injured? And more important how long will it be before I regain my memory?"

"That is what we are trying to find out," said the doctor. "Listen don't worry we have plenty of time to get you back to normal. It could take a few hours, a few days, and could be weeks before you regain your memory. But from my experience they all eventually regain their memory. Normally it takes a few days. I have to go now. I have other patients to take care of. I will be back later. You talk with Detective Bensen. It will all come back to you eventually." The doctor then left.

"Let's try to figure out who you are," said Robert. "What do you remember about your life? Do you remember where you were going? Do you remember any one in your family?"

"I don't remember where I was going," said the lady. "All I remember is waking up here. I don't know if I have any family. Oh Detective Bensen, what am I going to do?" she was again starting to get excited.

"Don't worry," said Robert. "I will never leave you. Please call me Robert. Consider me your friend and not a Detective. I will be with you until you regain all you memory back. I will work with you on this."

"Why would you do this?" asked the lady calming down at Robert promise.

"Because it's my joob and I like you." "You don't even know me," said the lady.

"I have been in this business for twenty five years I can figure out people's characteristics. I knew from the time you woke up before you knew you were injured and had lost your memory. It was when you said Hi and the expression on your face that gave you away. You are a kind and affectionate lady."

"That moment could be misleading," said the lady now with a small smile on her face. "I was attracted to you."

"And I am attracted to you also," said Robert, "and that would also prove my point. I would not be attracted to just anyone. Now, let's end all this fooling around. Let us start with what you can remember if anything. But before that, let's choose a name that we can call you until we find out you real name. Do you have any ideas of what you would like to be called?"

"I have no ideas," said the lady.

"Would you like Mary or Annie," said Robert.

"None of them sound like me," said the lady. "Why don't you just pick one and we will use it." Robert thought for a while then something popped into his head.

"You know what," said Robert. "When I was sitting here waiting for you to wake up you turned on your side and you started making a sound like a cat purring. So what name can that suggest?"

"I don't know," said the lady, "perhaps a name like Pricilla." "No, I know what we should call you. Since you acted like a cat let's call you Cathy. What do you think?"

"That is funny," said the lady with a smile on her face. "Let's go with Cathy."

"OK now Cathy," said Robert saying her name so that they both could get used to it. "Is there anything at all that you can remember?" "I think that I remember cooking," said Cathy. "I think I'm remembering a stove and a chocolate cake. Now I remember. It was my mother's recipe. I kind of remember my mother. She was a very good cook."

"Don't you see?" said Robert. "Just talking about anything will slowly bring back your memory."

Yes I see," said Cathy. "Now tell me about your life. Are you married? Do you have any children? I don't know anything about you. That may also trigger something in my memory."

"I don't have much to tell you," said Robert. "I grew up in Cleveland. I went to Cleveland State University. After graduating I went to the State Police Academy. I studied the various techniques in searching and finding evidence in criminal cases. Apparently I was good at it so that they assigned me as the Detective in the investigation office. Therefore they call me Detective Bensen. Yes I was married to my college sweetheart. She passed away two years ago. I have two children a boy and a girl." Does that answer your question?"

"Yes," said Cathy, "now I know more about you then you know about me." They both laughed. Just then the doctor walked in.

"How are you guys doing?" he asked looking more at Cathy. "I feel good," said Cathy.

"Where do we go from here?" asked Robert.

"Well we have to teach her body to eat again," said the doctor. "She has been fed intravenously till now. We have to feed her slowly. First we will feed her with soup and slowly with harder food. It will take a couple of days."

Robert visited Cathy every day to keep her company. It was on the third day that the doctor walked into the room with a smile on his face.

"Well," said the doctor. I find that you are perfecctly healthy. Therefore, I am releasing you this morning."

"Where am I going?" said Cathy showing an alarming expression. "I don't have a home to go to."

"Don't worry," broke in Robert. "It is my duty to take care of you. Gather up all your stuff and let's go."

"What stuff?" said Cathy getting more settled." All I have is the old clothes that are very filthy."

"You can take the hospital garments," said the doctor. A few minutes later, Robert placed Cathy in his car and started for home. They had no idea whaat surprises the future would bring.

## CHAPTER TWO

# THE LONG HAUL

O N THE WAY HOME, Robert called Captain Wilson
"Hi Captain. I have the client we call Cathy. She has been released from the hospital. She still doesn't remember anything.

"Can you bring her here?" asked the Captain.

"Her clothes are all dirty from the woods where she was found. She is currently wearing hospital garments. I would like to take her home first and let her get cleaned up"

"That's fine," said the Captain. "Don't take too long. It is our duty to find out who did this to her"

"I think she will want to takea shower and clean up a little," said Robert. "I may have to wash her clothes or perhaps she can fit into one of my wife's clothes that I have stored away since she passed. I will bring her in after lunch."

"Where do you think we could house her until we can find where she lives or find a relative," asked the captain. "I don't think a jail cell would be appropriate."

"I have an extra bed room that I could give her until we find a better place," suggested Robert. He already had that in mind since he met her.

"That will be fine," said the Captain and hung up. Robert drove home and pulled his car into the garage. He then helped Cathy out of the car and walked her into the family room.

"This is a very beautiful room," said Cathy. "I could spend many evenings here watching TV on this large TV set."

"I'm glad you like it," said Robert. "You can spend all the time you want here until we find out who you really are." He then led her up eight steps to the kitchen. "This is the kitchen. As you can see, through this doorway directly in front of you, is the dining room. To the left of the dining room is the living room." He then led her thought the open door way on their left. It led to the Living room. Just directly on the left as they entered the living room were the steps to the bedrooms. He led her up the stairs.

"Wow," said Cathy. "This hallway is like a bowling alley."

"The first room on your right is the TV room. My wife didn't like a TV in the main bedroom, so we made this room the TV room. As you can see it is very small and too small for a bedroom. The first room on your left is the main bedroom. It has a full bathroom off its far corner." As they walked down the hall, Robert continued, "Next on the left is Liana's bedroom. Across from it on your left is the main bathroom. Now down at the end of the hall on your rightis Tommy's bedroom. Across from it on your left is yoour bedroom." Robert then took her into the bedroom. "In the closet are several of my late wife's clothes. See if you can find one that fits and that you would like to wear. After you find one, take it and the robe and go into the main bathroom and take a shower. In the medicine cabinet you will find all the chemicals you woman like to wear. I will go down to the kitchen and make us a couple of sandwiches for lunch. I will also take your dirty clothes and put them in the washer. Don't take too long because I promised the captain that we will be in his office after lunch." With that instruction said Robert left and went down to the kitchen and made two hamburgers. He also put the dirty clothes in the washer. Cathy found a dress she liked that fit nicely and then took a shower. She then got dressed found a perfume she liked and finally came down stairs.

"How do I look?" asked Cathy turning around so that Robert could see the complete outfit she put on. She was wearing a black pair of jeans with a white blouse and a white colorfully spotted jacket.

"You look great," said Robert really impressed. "It never looked that good on Rita. By the way, I made a hamburger for each of us. I hope you like hamburgers and that one is enough."

"I don't remember if I like hamburgers. It looks great. I'm sure one is enough." They ate the hamburgers and some French fried potato that Robert had left from breakfast. It turned out that Cathy liked the hamburgers. After they ate they drove to the police station and entered the Captain's office.

"Great to see you two," said the Captain. "We have to start the process of finding your identity and communicate with any family members you may have. I'm sure they are worried sick at your absence." "What process are you talking about?" asked Cathy looking worried.

"Don't worry," said the Captain. "There is no pain involved except if we take some blood to see if we can match your DNA with a family. We are committed to find out who you are and get you home." Next the Captain called his secretary. "Amanda, Is the photographer here yet?"

"Yes" said Amanda, "He is waiting for you to call him."

"Bring him in," said the Captain. The photographer walked in with all his equipment, ready to take pictures of the young lady. It only took ten minutes and he had all the pictures they needed. Next he had another officer take her finger prints.

"Howcan my finger prints help find who I am?" asked Cathy. "We are going to use every angle," said the Captain. "We never know if you have been finger printed to prove your identity somewhere." Smiling he added, "We never know you may be an escape criminal." Next a nurse came in and took a sample of Cathy's blood. "We are all done now," said the captain. "We will have this information out in action. We will have the picture posted in all our usual places. If someone recognizes you we will contact you. So you can leave now and have a great day." Robert and Cathy were happy to leave. They went straight home. That evening when the girls came home Robert introduced Cathy to them. He then introduced his Kids.

"Liana is my daughter and Amy is my unofficial adopted daughter." Amy then explained all that had happened to her.

"Now I understand why you Robbie are so good to me," said Cathy, "You are a gentle kind hearted angel."

That Sunday Robert took Cathy to church. Before they got there he explained about the heavenly father and his son Jesus. At church he introduced her to the pastor. She did mention that she had a feeling that she had been to church before. She said that she felt at home there.

They spent the next three days sitting around, talking about anything that came up hoping that it would remind Cathy of anything in her life. They sometimes watched TV. The thing thhat surprised everyone was that when they first got home Cathy went into the kitchen and cooked a delicious dinner.

"How did you know how to cook?" asked Robert, "and such a delicious dinner."

"I don't know," said Cathy. "I just did what came into my mind. I think I loved to cook. Maybe I was a chef before I got hurt." Cathy continued to cook dinner every night except Friday when it was Roberts turn to cook. No one cooked salmon like Robert did.

"Will miracles never end," said Liana one evening after dinner. Amy and Liana both loved the dinners that were prepared for them every night. They all enjoyed the company of Cathy. It was like they were all part of the same family. It was four days later that Robert called Captain Wilson.

"Good morning Captain," said Robert. "What is going on? Have you heard anything about our young lady?"

"No," said the Captain. "We have had no reaction. We have only sent out information and picture here locally. I am planning to send it out all over the Midwest. Perhaps she is not from this area. Let's wait a few more days before we take more drastic action." Robert wondered what the Captain meant by more drastic action.

The next several days were very delightful. Robert decided that they should enjoy the time they had together.

"What do we do now?" asked Cathy after they had eaten breakfast. "It may take a month before we get an answer to my problem."

"I think we should enjoy the time we have together," said Robert, saying aloud what he was thinking. "We don't know if you are married. If you are married we would probably not see each other again. I enjoy being with you. First let me take you around this area. Perhaps seeing the area will bring back some of your memory."

"What do you have in mind?" asked Cathy.

"Let me take you first to the Akron Art Museum," suggested Robert. "I have not been there for years. I used to like to do some picture painting."

"I know," said Cathy. "I have seen some of you painnting around your house."

"How did you know they were my paintings?" asked Robert being puzzled by her statement.

"I looked at the bottom left at the name of the artist," said Cathy. "I saw your name on most of the ones you have hanging in your house." "You are smarter then I gave you credit for," said Robert. "Why do you look to see who the artist was," asked Robert. "Perhaps you are somehow affiliated with some art society."

"I have no idea," said Cathy. "So let's go. Maybe being there will remind me of any affiliations I may have with art." An hour later they arrived at the Akron Art museum. Cathy seemed thrilled at seeing all the wonderful paintings. When they got through they headed home.

"Well," asked Robert, "what do you think?"

"I'm so glad that you brought me there," said Cathy. "I enjoyed it very much. However, it did not bring back any memories."

"Well," said Robert, "the effort is not over. It just started." That afternoon Robert took Cathy to the Akron Zoo. They enjoyed it but Robert admitted that it was nowhere as exciting as the Cleveland Zoo. Robert promised Cathy that he would take her to the Cleveland Zoo on Saturday. On Wednesday Robert brought her to Fort Island Park. They enjoyed the walk through the park. They also sat on the benches and enjoyed watching the tennis players play their games. That evening Cathy enjoyed telling the girls about their time at the park. Cathy mentioned that their dad was going to take her to the Cleveland Zoo.

"We want to go too," said Liana. "We have never been to the Cleveland Zoo. We hear that it is amazing."

"If you can get off from work you are welcome to come with

us," said Robert." On Thursday Robert drove Cathy to the Cleveland Natural History Museum. Cathy was thrilled at all she saw. While they were in the neighborhood they also stopped at the Cleveland Art museum. Cathy was thrilled.

"Wow, she said when they decided to leave. "This is at least ten times more exciting than the one in Akron." On the way home Robert decided since it was still early that he would stop and visit his parents.

"You know Cathy," said Robert. "It is still early. I think we should stop at my parent's house. I would like you to meet them. I have mentioned you on my phone calls to them and they would be thrilled to meet you."

"I would like to meet them too, but I am very nervous. I hope they will like me."

"Don't worry," said Robert. "Theywill like you because I am bringing you to see them. I have not brought many girls to meet them." "Why me?" said Cathy. "What are you doing? Remember I may be married."

"Do you mean that I can't have married friends," said Robert. "Anyway I think you have to meet people so that you can feel like you are part of society. I've had a feeling that you think that you are not part of this world. That is why I like to keep you entertained and busy with people. Don't my girls make you feel like you are part of the family?"

"Are you a psychiatrist doctor playing like a police man?" said Cathy with a smile on her face. "You are reading my mind." A few minutes later they arrived at Robert's parent house. When Robert's mom saw them she embraced Robert.

"Sweetheart," she said with love in her voice, "It's so good to see you. It seems like it's been forever since the last time we saw you."

"Hi mom," said Robert. "It is nice to see you too. I want you to meet the young lady I told you about. We call her Cathy until we find out what her real name is."

"Hi," said Robert's mother as she hugged her. "It is so good to meet you."

"It is also a pleasure to meet you Mrs. Bensen," said Cathy. "Come on in and make you at home," said Robert's mom. She grabbed Cathy by the hand and brought her into the living room.

"Please call me Liana." He said to her.

"Where is Dad?" asked Robert looking around for his dad.

"He was called into work. Although he is retired they call him in once in a while to help. He should be home very soon."

"I guess he is like me," said Robert. "I am retired but I am also called to help once in a while. Cathy is one of those special assignments."

"How long can you stay? Will you stay for dinner?"

"Sorry mom," said Robert, "We have to get home. The girls don't know where we are. We have to get home and make dinner for them." "I would love to meet Amy and of course I would like to see my granddaughter too," said Robert's mom.

"Well maybe you can see them this Saturday," said Robert. "We are going to visit the Cleveland Zoo. The girls said that they wanted to come with us. We can stop on the way home as we did today."

"That would be great," said Robert's mother. "You will have to stop here and have dinner. I will not take no for an answer."

"I don't know mom," said Robert. "I don't want to put you out. Don't forget there will four of us. There will be six including you and dad. That is a lot to handle in such a short time."

"It would give me a great pleasure," said Robert's mom. "It will be like we were having another holiday. I will start the dinner arrangement tomorrow. You better come. If you don't come I will have a diner for six go to waste. I am going to start buying needed things as soon as your father gets back."

"All right mom," said Robert. "We will be here. What do you think Cathy?"

"I can't wait until Saturday," said Cathy.

"That's great," said Robert's mom. "Now what can I get you? Would you like a soda or perhaps a piece of pie that I baked just yesterday? It is Tom's favorite."

"Thanks mom," said Robert, "but I don't want anything now. It would spoil my dinner with the girls.

"Do you want anything Cathy," asked Robert's mom. "I don't need anything, thank you Mrs. Bensen."

"Won't you two at least have a cup of coffee?" asked Robert's mother.

"All right if it will make you happy," said Cathy, "I will have a cup of coffee."

"What would you like in your coffee?" asked Robert's mother. "Would you like some milk and some sugar?"

"I don't know," said Cathy. "I don't have any idea on what I would like in my coffee."

"I know what," said Robert's mother. "Let me put some Coffee Mate in it. I guarantee you will love it. I can't drink coffee without it. How about you Robbie, what will you have?"

"I'll pass, mom," said Robert.

"Let's go sit in the kitchen whileI make the coffee," said Robert's mom. "There we could talk while I make the coffee." They quickly moved to the kitchen and sat down around the table.

"We can't stay too long," said Robert.

"Cathy," said Robert's mom, "have you gained any of your memory back yet?"

"All I can remember is a little of my mother and a few dinners she taught me to cook. I can't remember the name of the meals but I instinctively can put everything together." They sat a while drinking the coffee conversing in some small talk.

"I'm sorry mom," said Robert, "but we have to go. We have to prepare a dinner for the girls. They are pretty hungry when they get home." They all hugged each other saying good bye and Robert and Cathy sadly left. On the way home Robert opened the conversation.

"Cathy, did anything to day bring back any memory?"

"I think it mostly brought me very wonderful new memories. It reminded me how important family is."

"Then it all was worth it," said Robert.

"You can bet on that. Your mother is a very wonderful loving mother."

"You will see more of how sweet she is Saturday," added Robert.

They soon got home and immediately started dinner. After dinner the girls surrounded Cathy and wanted to know everything she had done that day.

The next day was Friday. After breakfast Cathy asked Robert, "What is on the agenda today?" she asked.

"I think we need a little rest," said Robert. "We will need all our energy for tomorrow. It is going to be a full day. However tonight if you like we can go to Bicentennial Park. They have a different band playing there every night. Tonight they have a 1950 era music festival. If you girls want to go we can bring a blanket and sit on the grass and listen to the music. We can bring some crackers and cheese."

"That sounds like a delightful evening," said Cathy." How about you girls do you want to come?"

"No way," said Lianaa. "That is not my kind of music." "How about you Amy?" asked Robert.

"I think I will pass," said Amy.

"Alright then," said Robert, "it will be just you and me Cathy." With that said they each went their own way. Amy and Liana decided to go to the mall and look around at what was available they might like. Robert and Cathy sat down and watched some TV. The day went by quickly and it was soon evening. Robert and Cathy got all they needed and Robert drove to the police station. To park at the park's parking lot was usually a major problem. It was not large enough for the audience that attended the affair. However since Robert was a part time member of the police force he could park at the police station parking lot. The park was across the street of the police station. Robert and Cathy were soon sitting on their blanket ready to watch the band play. The music started exactly at eight o'clock. It was the exact type of music Robert loved. Cathy seemed to enjoy it also. The music lasted until eleven o'clock. Robert and Cathy were sorry it was over.

"Well I hope it was your type of music," said Robert as they got up to leave.

"I'm not sure what type of music is my favorite," said Cathy. "I just know that I enjoyed this evening's music very much. At this moment it is my favorite since I have not heard any of the other types of music."

"Very well said," answered Robert, "now let us go to bed."

The next morning they all got up early excited with the thought of going to the Cleveland Zoo. They barely ate breakfast and were soon on the way to the zoo. It took about an hour to get there. The traffic was very heavy being the time most people go to work. When they got there Robert paid for the tickets and thy proceeded to enter into the zoo area. After hesitation at a few cages they came to the gorilla cage. They look at the gorillas and they all kept on going to the next cage. Robert was just feet ahead of Cathy. Cathy stopped at the screen that held the gorillas from exiting the area. One of the gorillas came up to the screen that separated them and looked straight at Cathy. Cathy looked straight at the gorilla.

"Robbie," yelled Cathy, "what are you doing in there? Get out of there. The gorillas are dangerous."Robert heard her and yelled back

"Very funny," said Robert with a big smile on his face. "I guess you at least have your humor back."

"Oh Robbie," said Cathy. "You are out here. I thought that was you in there." By then Cathy and the girls were laughing hysterically.

"All right guys," said Robert. "You had your fun. I wonder how hard you girls will laugh when I leave without you."

"Oh Daddy," said Liana, "you are too good hearted to do that." They spent the rest of the day reviewing the rest of the zoo with high humor. When it was about five o'clock they decided to leave and go to the Roberts parent's house. Although they did not see the entire zoo, they felt they had to leave. When they got to Robert's parent's house there his mother met them at the door.

"Hi Robbie," she said as she hugged him. She then turned to Liana and hugged her. She did the same thing to Amy and Cathy. "Come on inside," she said. "Cathy it is so good to see you again. And who is this lovely young lady?" she said when she hugged Amy. "This is the young girl I told you about," said Robert.

"Her name is Amelia. We all call her Amy." Just then a young man walked into the room.

"Tommy," yelled Robert. "What are you doing here?"

"I only work mornings on Saturday. Grandma told me of your plans for today so I thought I would come and meet my new sister and your friend Cathy."

"I'm so glad to see you," said Robert. "This is Amy, thhe young girl I told you about. And this is Cathy. It is my job to find out who she is."

Tommy shook hands with them and then hugged Liana. "How are you Sis?"

"Come sit at the table," said Roberts mother. "Dinner will be ready in about a half hour."

"Where is Dad," asked Robert looking around. Before she could answer Robert's dad walked into the room.

"Hi everyone," he said as he looked at the guests, "and who are these charming young ladies?"

"Of course you know your granddaughter," said Robert. "This one here next to me is the one we call Cathy. The other one sitting next to Liana is Amy. She is the one that lives with us until college starts. Cathy is the one that lost her memory. She has no idea of where she lives or if she has any family. She is in my charge until we can find out who she is. Our agency has her picture displayed all over Ohio. I hope we will find out who she is."

"Hi Liana, Hi Tommy," said Robert's dad.

"Enough of that," said Robert's mother as she started bring in the salad. "It is time to eat."

"Grandma," said Liana as she got up and helped her grandmother bring in the salad plates for each at the table. Amy got up to help too. "I would like to help." They both helped.

"When you finish your salad I will bring in the main meal," said Robert's mother. "And Robbie, I have made your favorite diner. I have made Cavatelli with meat balls and pork neck bones." They all enjoyed the dinner. After dinner they talked a while and then Robert's mother brought in the dessert. She had made strawberry pie. When they finished the dessert they all had a cup of coffee and sat to talk.

"Now tell me all the things you saw at the Cleveland zoo," said Robert's mother." Liana did most of the talking although the others added their description all the time. They were having a very enjoyable time together. Unfortunate time went by too fast. It soon was eleven.

"I'm sorry to break this up but it is getting late and we must leave. We have to go to church tomorrow. With many hugus, they all were feeling sorrowful to leave but also a feeling that they had a very enjoyable evening.

The next morning after breakfast they went to church. The preacher gave a sermon that Robert felt was close to home. It was just what Cathy needed. He talked about how tohandle life events that seem to be unexplainable. He talked about difficult ordeals that could suddenly arise unexpectedly. He said that strange things may occur to any of us that seem uncorrectable. Have faith. Give the lord time and all things will comme together for good. Faith is the cure for all problems. After the seermon Robert turned to Cathy.

"What did you think of the sermon?" He asked.

"I think that God meant it for me. I will have to have faith. After all God sent me you."

"I believe that all your problems will end joyfully," said Robert. "That reminds me of my answer years ago when a friend asked why God was allowing bad things happen to him. I told him that I love my daughter Liana with all my heart. But as she grew up I gave her more freedom. One day we were walking through the park and Liana tripped on a rock and fell skinning her knee. I didn't make her fall. I didn't want her to fall. I didn't make her fall. She was old enough to walk by herself. However, I was there to pick her up and mended her knee. That is the way God is with us. He gave us all the freedom but he will be there to help you when you need it."

"You know Dad," responded Amy. "You should have been a preacher."

"Very funny," said Robert.

"You may think it is funny but I am serious. You are a great Christian."

"I pray daily that all of you are great Christians." When they got home they had lunch. Robert cooked Filet Minion on the grill. They all enjoyed the dinner with great appreciation. After they finished eating, Robert got a phone call. It was his sister Teresa. After a few minutes talking he hung up.

"Oh girls," said Robert. "I forgot that Wednesday is the fourth of July. My sister has invited us to her house for the celebration as she has done every year."

"Why is it a yearly thing for her?" asked Cathy.

"It is not a yearly thing for her," responded Robert. "It is a yearly thing for us. Let me explain. My sister's housesits at the edge of the country club golf course. At the end of her lot is a hill that looks down at a small river. Across the river is a grove of trees. On the other side of the trees is where they have the Fourth of July fireworks. My sister usually gets a couple of large pizzas and we eat in the patio. At about ten we carry folding chairs to the end of the lot and watch the fireworks."

"I can hardly wait," said Cathy. "I don't remember if I ever saw fireworks."

"Do you know what a fireworks is?" asked Robert.

"That is the strange thing," said Cathy. "I know exactly what it is but I don't remember ever seeing one. That is like a lot of things I know about although I don't remember doing them. There are other things like the English language. How come I can remember it?"

Monday and Tuesday went by quickly. Robert and Cathy spent time relaxing and watching TV. Cathy insisted that she do all the cooking. The kids came home about five and they all ate together. Wednesday was the holiday and the girls were home. The day seemed to go on forever. Finally it was five o'clock. Robert's sister had invited them to there at five. They made sure they were not late. When they got there Teresa welcomed them with great affection. Tommy was already there.

"Theresa," started Robert. "This is my client who lost her memory. We call her Cathy"

"Welcome," said Teresa. "I'm so happy that you could join with us. We love to have you." With that said she hugged her.

"And this is Amy," continued Robert. "This is the young lady I told you about on the phone over a month ago. I explained about her problem."

"Hi Amy," said Teresa. "I'm so glad you could come." She then hugged her. "And of course, I know Liana. It is so good to see you. It's been too long" With that said she hugged her. She then turned to Robert. She hugged him without saying a word. She was too moved. The girls all embraced Tommy. They were glad that he was there with them. Teresa then grabbed Liana by the hand. "Come on in all of you. We are going out to the patio. I have two large boxes of pizza."

"I can hardly wait," said Robert. "I can remember how fantastic the pizza was that you had last year." They sat around the table Teresa had in the patio and enjoyed the pizza.

"Wow," said Ammy, "Daddy wasn't exaggerating about the pizza" "You call him Daddy," asked Teresa, "that is so sweet."

"The help that he has given me is more than most real dads generally do for their real children." Teresa and the girls sat around answering question about their individual lives until it was near nine o'clock.

"I think we had better go to the rear end of my land," said Teresa. "I think the fireworks are about to begin." They each grabbed a folding chair and moved to the end of the lot. There were two trees that were at the end of the property. On the other side of the trees the land slopped down to a river. They set up their chairs on the top of the hill. On the other side of the river, about five hundred feet, were a group of trees. It was on the other side of the trees that the fireworks took place. Robert had brought four of his own chairs. He was not sure if his sister had invited others to view the fireworks. He wanted to be sure he and his girls had a place to sit. It turned out that Teresa had not invited anyone else. It was less than a minute after they had all settle down that the fireworks started. At first it was one large rocket with a large booming explosion. Then every few seconds it was followed with several rockets exploding into a beautiful array of color. Each rocket was of different color and shapes. This went on for about forty five minutes. Suddenly a burst of several rockets filled the sky all at the same time with all different colors and went on for about five minutes. Then everything went silent.

"I think it is over," said Teresa. Robert and the girls goto up to fold there chair when suddenly another rocket was fired into the sky. Then everything went on as it had happened at the beginning. Every few seconds another rocket would be shot into the air. They all sat down again to watch as before.

"That is very unusual," said Teresa. "It never happened like this before. They must have forgotten an array of rockets."

"That's fine," said Robert. "Let's enjoy it." It continued for about ten minutes. Then the endingarray was repeated. This time it was the end.

"That was the greatest fireworks I ever saw," said Amy. "I have seen several in my life time and none were anywhere as good as this one."

"What do you think Cathy?" asked Robert.

"I think it was fantastic," said Cathy. "However, I don't remember seeing another one to make comparison." Everyone laughed realizing that Cathy was making a joke out of it. After they all made a few comment on the firework display Robert decided that they had to go home.

"I'm afraid that we have to leave now," said Robert. "The girls have to go to work tomorrow and Cathy and I need a little rest."

"Can't you stay for a little dessert and a cup of coffee?" said Teresa. "Come on Robbie. I don't get to see you and the kids often. Make an exception this time only. Do it for me."

"All right," said Robert. Then turning to the girls he continued. "How about you girls, what do you think? Do you want to stay a little longer? It's a little after eleven." All the girls said yes. They wanted to stay and have coffee and dessert. Teresa made coffee and brought out an apple pie. After they had dessert and coffee Robert got up.

"I'm afraid we have to go," said Robert. "It is almost midnight. You girls are going to suffer tomorrow morning." They all got up hugged each other with love in their faces and Robert and the girls finally left. When they got home they immediately went to bed.

The next morning when Robert got up he found that Liana and Amy had already left for work. He went down stairs to start breakfast. He had no sooner gotten out the frying pan when he heard a sound behind him.

"Good morning," said Cathy. "I see that you got up before me. I guess the girls are all gone to work."

"I just got up," said Robert. "I guess the girls were not as tired as I though. I can tell that they had a bowl of cereal and left."

"What do you plan for today?" asked Cathy.

"I don't have anything planned," said Robert. "Do you have anything you would like to do?"

"If you don't have anything planned," said Cathy, "I would like it if you drop me off at the mall. I would like to see what is available and spend a little time there."

"That will be fine with me," said Robert, "But if you like something how will you pay for it?"

"You can lend me some money," said Cathy. "I promise to pay you back when I recover from my problem. Anyway I just want to wander around a bit."

Well," said Robert. "I think I have about two hundred in cash. You can have that as a backup."

"Thank you," said Cathy. "I will most likely bring it back to you." "Why don't you buy yourself some clothes? You don't have any of your own."

"The clothes of your wife that you let me borrow are more than I need for now," responded Cathy.

"Alright then," said Robert, "go get ready and I'll drop you off." It only took about ten minutes and Cathy came down.

"Do we set a time for you to pick me up?" asked Cathy.

"That is not necessary. Here is my phone number," said Robert handing her a piece of paper. "Any of the stores will let you use their phone to call me."

"By the way, I borrowed one of your wife's empty purses," said Cathy as she put the note in the purse. "I hope you don't mind."

"You can have it permanently, or as long as you need it." Robert and Cathy got into Robert's car and Robert dropped her off at the entrance to Macy's.

"When you are ready to come home and call me, please be at this same entrance. I will pick you up here." With that said Robert left for home.

It was after four in the afternoon when Robert got a call from Cathy.

"I am ready to coome home," said Cathy. "Come and get me." "I'll be right there," said Robert. He then got into his car and went to pick her up. She was right where he had told her to be. She quickly got into the car.

"You were there a lot longer than I expected," said Robert. "I was worried about you. Where did you have lunch?"

"I didn't have any lunch," said Cathy. "I hope you have a big supper ready."

"Fortunately it will be ready in about a half hour. The girls will be home about four thirty. I am cooking salmon for dinner." They got home before the girls did. Robert set up the fish ready to cook. He always waited for the girls to get home. As soon as they entered the door he put the fish in the oven and set the broiler on and set the timer. It takes about ten minutes to cook. Robert cooked the fish for six minutes on one side and after six minutes he took it out, turned the fish over spread his special mixture he made for fish, then sprinkled some paprika over it and then put it back in the oven. He then broiled it for five minutes more. They all enjoyed the dinner. Everyone loved Robert's fish dinners. He sometimes cooked Tilapia the same way.

The next day was Friday. After they all ate breakfast and the girls went to work Robert and Cathy relaxed in the family room.

"What do you want to do today?" Robert asked Cathy knowing that she was about to ask the same question.

"If you have no other plan," said Cathy, "I would like you to take me to Giant Eagle. Today is Friday. I want to buy some groceries for the weekend. I think I remember some very delicious recipe. I want to do the cooking the next two or three days."

"Wow," said Robert, "where did that come from?"

"I want to do something around here," said Cathy. "You don't even get out of the car. You can take a magazine with you and read while I do the shopping. I don't want you in there with me."

"How are you going to pay for the food that you buy?" asked Robert really kidding her.

"Well I believe thaat you are going to lend me your credit card," said Cathy with a smile on her face.

"All right," said Robert. "It isn't necessary for me to come with you. You are smart enough to be trusted. "I can give you my credit card and you can borrow my car."

"Good," said Cathy. "I can go right after lunch." Cathy did not waste any time to go to the grocery store. It was after three that she got back. Robert helped her bring the food in from the car trunk. It filled the refrigerator.

"Did you buy out the whole store?" asked Robert.

"It didn't cost me anything," said Cathy. "So I bought all that I wanted."

"Very funny," said Robert. "You have a strange sense of humor."

"I hope you have no plans for tomorrow," said Cathy, "and I hope it doesn't rain. I have some special food for a nice picnic. I picked Saturday so the girls can come with us." That evening Cathy made a meal that was fabulous. All that they knew was that it had some sausage in it. Liana said that she recognized the dinner. She called it sausage casserole. They all enjoyed it with great thankfulness.

The next day was Saturday. Cathy made some fantastic sandwiches and fruit salad and they went to Sand Run Metropolitan Park. They found a nice grassy area and set down a large blanket on the ground. There the girls threw around a beach ball they had brought with them. At lunch time they sat on the blanket and ate the lunch Cathy had prepared for them. After lunch Robert and Cathy sat on the blanket and relaxed. The girls went back to playing with their ball. It was about five thirty when they decided to leave the park. On the way home Robert stopped at the Olive Garden for dinner. The day was enjoyed by all. On the way home they all expressed their happy feelings

"I cannot imagine ever having this much fun in all my live," said Cathy. "I don't know how I will ever be able to leave you guys."

"You will always be welcoome here," said Robert. "Even if we find that you have a husband and children, then you can bring them with you and we will have a day together." No more was said after that. They all wished privately that she was single and would eventually move in with them.

Sunday they all went to church. The preacher gave a fantastic sermon. After the sermon on the way home Cathy expressed her feelings "You know," said Cathy. "I feel like I belong in this church and at least this religion. I heartily believe in all that is preached here. I am sure that when I get my memory back I will remember that I am a Born Again Christian."

"If you were not then you are now," said Robert. That evening went by as usual. The girls went upstairs to the upstairs TV room and Robert and Cathy stayed in the Family Room and watched a romantic movie.

It was the next day, after breakfast, after the girls had left for work, and after Robert and Cathy sat down to relax that the telephone rang. It was Captain Wilson.

"Hi Captain," said Robert. "What's up?"

"We have heard from the Brook Park Police Department," said Captain Wilson. "They have a driver's license that has a picture that resembles the girl whose picture we put out for recognition." The Captain then gave him the telephone number of the police station in Brook Park. Robert did not hesitate to call the Police Station.

"Hello," he said when someone answered the phone. "My name is Lieutenant Benson of the Fairlawn Police Department."

"This is Sergeant Torino. I understand that you have a young lady that has lost her memory. How soon can you get her here? We would like to compare signatures and blood type to make sure it is her."

"I can bring her there right now," said Robert. "I would like to get this over as soon as possible."

"Great I'll be waiting for you," said Sergeant Torino. He then gave Robert the address and direction on how to get to his station. Robert then turned to Cathy.

"A police station in Cleveland thinks they may have information that could help identify you," said Robert." So go and get ready. I told them we would come as soon as possible."

"I will be ready in about five minutes," said Cathy as she left for her bedroom. About five minutes later she came down.

"You look fantastic," said Robert. "You are not going to a party. You didn't have to get all dressed up just to go to a police station."

"I don't have any clothes of my own," said Cathy. "Thanks to your wife's closet I have something to wear." They then got into Robert's ten thirty. Entering inside Robert walked to the front desk and spoke to the officer that was behind the desk.

"We are here to see Sergeant Torino. Can you tell him we are here?"

"You must be Lieutenant Benson," said the officer. "Please follow me." He then led them to Sergeant Torino's office. When the Sergeant saw them at the door way he spoke out to them.

"Please come in and sit down. I think we have a match. You look like the picture on this driver's license." He said as he looked at Cathy. "However, I will need more evidence. So if you don't mind I will have you go with Officer Jones. She will get your finger prints and a sample of your blood."

"Before I go can I see the driver's license?" asked Cathy. "Of course," said the Sergeant handing her the license.

"I see that the name on it is Loretta James," said Cathy.

"Now go with Officer Jones. I will explain everything after you come back," said the Sergeant. "I don't want to give out information if it isn't you."

"I understand," said Cathy. The Sergeant then got on his phone and called in the girl he call Vicky. When she came in the Sergeant introduced her to Robert and Cathy and they left to go into the station's lab.

"Now Lieutenant Bensonn," said theSergeant, "tell me what you know of this case."

"Well, some young kids found her in the wood in our area and called our office. Onne of our officers went, and seeing the ladies condition called an ambulance. That was when I got assigned to the case. She was in the hospital over two weeks in a coma. When she came to, she couldn't even remember her name."

"Did she remember anything?" asked the sergeant. "Did she realize that she had a problem?"

"Not right away," said Robert, "she only realized that she had a problem when we asked her name. She laid there in awe that she couldn't tell us her name."

"She seemed pretty normal at this time," said the sergeant. "Has she given you any problem due to her inability to remember anything?" "No in fact she has been very happy," said Robert. "We took her in with me and my two daughters and they all got along like she was part of our family." Just then Cathy, now being called Lorrie, came into the office.

"I have given all the information to Doctor Evens," said Officer Jones. "He said he will give us the information in about two hours. His initial indication is that the two are the same."

"Well since we have some time," said Lorrie, "tell us what you can as to how you got the articles you have."

"Listen," said the sergeant. "The answers that I am looking for will be here in about an hour. Why don't you two go out and have some lunch near here and comeback in about two hours? There are a few fine restaurants on Holland Road. I will then sit with you and give you every detail of the case."

"Sounds like a good idea," said Robert. "Let's go Cathy or should

I start calling you Lorrie?" As they got in the car Lorrie turned to Robert.

"Why is he so afraid to give us any information?" she asked.

"I think he is sticking to the law. He cannot give information about anyone other than the involved party."

"Look there," said Lorrie. "That looks like a nice place to have lunch."

"Where ever you want to stop,"said Robert as he pulled up to a parking space. "At least this place has a parking space in front." As they walked into the restaurant a waitress met them at the front door.

"How can I help you?" she asked. "Do you want a takeout or do you want to eat here?"

"We would like to have lunch here, said Robert." The waitress then led them to an empty table. She then handed them each a menu. They each placed an order and then began to discuss what was happening.

"I am going to find it hard to call you Lorrie instead of Cathy," said Robert. "I know Cathy, but I don't know Lorrie."

"Do you really believe that I am really Loretta?" asked Lorrie. "The sergeant seems to have doubts that I am."

"He is just being conscientious," said Robert. "He just wants to be one hundred percent sure."

"I wish he had told us a little about who I am," said Lorrie. "I am so nervous. I wonder if I have any relatives and most important do I have a husband?"

"We will know in just a few minutes," said Robert. The waitress then brought them their food. They ate silently. Nothing was said until they finished and got into the car.

"I am so nervous," said Lorrie. "I'm so worried that I won't like who I really am."

"I would not worry," said Robert. "I've known you for several weeks. Your personality would not change just because you lost your memory. I can tell you without a doubt that you are a sweet, kind, and loving person."

"Thank you," said Lorrie. "You are so kind. I think you just described your personality." They both smiled at her comment. They soon arrived at the Police Station. As soon as they got into the door they were lead to the sergeant's office.

"Please sit down," said the sergeant. "I have good news for you. All the information is in. The finger prints and the blood match. They are all yours. Therefore, I tell you that you are Loretta James. Your home is in Hobart Indiana. That is about fifteen miles south of Gary Indiana.

"Please tell us all that you know of me," asked Lorrie getting anxious."

"All right," said the sergeant. "A couple of week ago we got a phone call from the car rental agency at the airport. We sent an officer there to see what the problem was. They said that they had rented a car to a young lady and she was to return it in a couple of days. When she didn't return it we used our 'On Star' locations system and found the car in our parking lot. There they found the car with a purse on the front seat and a luggage in the back seat and the trunk. We have brought them here and checked the car for other evidence. That's where we found the blood on the back seat. We have looked through the purse and the attaché case. We found some documents containing excellent history of your job as an assistant nurse to a surgical Doctor named Dr. Ronald James. One interesting thing we found was that a few of the document list you as Mrs. Ronald James."

"I have a husband named Ronald and he is a doctor," asked Lorrie. "Have you tried to locate him?"

"When we first got this information we tried to call him from the phone we found in your belongings," said the sergeant. "They said that the phone was not in operation. We have found no other information." "I wonder why he has not tried to find her," said Robert. "He must have been aware of where she was going."

"I think you will have to find this out when she is taken home," said the sergeant.

"Have you any other information as to what might have happen at the airport where all this started?"

"What we figured happened is that as Mrs. James got out at the airport and after renting a car she was attacked by a thief who stole her money and perhaps her credit card. He must have hit her when she resisted and drove her to the woods where he dumped her."

"Well I guess we may never know," said Robert.

"Are you willing to take over this case?" asked the sergeant. "Yes," said Robert. "We will take full responsibility from here on." "Then I would like you to signthis release document," said the sergeant to Robert. "I also want you Mrs. James, to sign these papers that we have released to you the purse, the attaché case, and the suitcase that we found in the trunk of the rental car."" As Robert signed his paper Lorrie signed all her papers. Then the Sergeant turned over to them the purse, the attaché case and the large suitcase.

"Thank you so much Sergeant Torino," Said Robert and Lorrie at the same time. Robert then helped Lorrie with her suitcase and they went out to the car. Robert put the suitcase and Attaché case in the trunk of his car. Lorrie got into the front seat and Robert was about to get in the driver's seat when Officer Vicky ran out to them.

"Please don't leave," she said. "Sergeant Torino wants to see you for new information he just obtained."

"What information did he get?" asked Robert.

"I don't know," said Vicky. "He just yelled to me to stop you before you leave." Robert and Lorrie then follow her back into Sergeant Torino's office.

"I'm sorry to put this strain on you but I didn't want you to go all the way to Akron and then have to come back tomorrow."

"What is this all about?" asked Robert being puzzled by the whole situation.

"Well," said the sergeant, "when we first got into this we were not sure that a credit card was taken. We didn't even know if she had one. But to be sure we put out a notice to all the businesses in the area. However we just got a call from a local groceries store. The Officer I sent and a person using a credit card with Loretta James name on it was just arrested. They are on the way here. They will be here is about ten minutes."

"What could I do? No matter even if it was my father I would not recognize him," said Lorrie.

"Well let's see what happens," said Sergeant Torino. A few minutes later Officer Vicky entered the door.

"Sergeant," she said, "Bill is here with the fellow you want to talk to."

"Send them in," said the sergeant. The police officer with a young man walked into the office. Suddenly Lorrie looked shocked. She looked like she was very scared of the fellow that was brought in. She never got to say a word when the young man they brought in yelled out.

"Oh dear Lord," he said with a shocked tone to his voice. "You are alive. Thank heavens. I thought I had killed you. I'm so sorry. I did not mean to hurt you." Tears then showed up in his eyes.

"Do you recognize him?" asked Robert. "You seem like you were shocked when you saw him."

"I don't understand why," answered Lorrie. "It just came from my stomach. Perhaps my body recognizes him."

"Now then let's hear more," said Sergeant Torino to the young man. "Your name is Gordon Holland. Tell us what happened."

"I lost my job," started Gordon. "The company I worked for went out of business. I had been looking for a new job. I went to the Cleveland Airport to see if I could get a janitors job. They had no opening. I got a call from my employment agent that there was a possible job at the Copley High School as a janitor. I got into my car and found that I didn't know if I had enough gas to get to Copley. I got very upset, to put it mildly. I was hungry. I had not eaten for two days. I had no more money so when I saw this woman got into her car I decided to get money from her. I asked her nicely but she refused to help me. Then I pulled out my gun and tried to force her to give me her money. She looked like she was getting out of the car but instead when she was part way out she open the door quickly and hit me knocking theh gun from my hand. We both then fought for the gun. I don't know why because the gun was empty. I don't remember exactly what happen. I must have hit her with the handle part of the gun. The next thing I remember was that she was lying on the ground with a river of blood coming out of her head. I thought I had killed her so I shoved her in the back seat of her car which had enough gas to get me there and so I headed for Copley in her car. When I almost got there I saw the woods so I shoved her there and took off for Copley. I didn't get the job so I headed back to the Cleveland Airport. When I got there I saw the ladies purse on the floor on the passenger's side. I found about two hundred dollars and I took them and the credit card. I did not expect to use the credit card. I thought that with the two hundred dollars I could get along until I got a job. I first got gas for my car and left her car in the Cleveland parking lot where I first took it. Soon I ran out of money and since I had not gotten a job I used the credit card. So you know the rest. I am so sorry lady," he said turned to Lorrie. "I got desperate." Lorrie couldn't say a word. She didn't know what to say anyway.

"Well I think that covers everything," said Sergeant Torino. "Does anyone have any questions?"

"How soon can I take Lorrie home to Indiana?" asked Robert. "Don't do it for a while," Let's see what the judge has to say about this young man. I will call you after he has been seen by the judge."

Robert and Lorrie then left the police station. On the way home Lorrie opened up to Robert.

"I am such a mess," said Lorrie. "If I am married why hasn't he tried to find me? It sounds like it is not a happy marriage. I wish they had not found out who I am. I was so happy being with you and the girls."

"Just relax," said Robert. "This is the most important time that you have to have faith and trust in the Lord. He will take care of you. Also listen to me. I care very much about you. I will never let you go through anything alone."

"Thank you," said Lorrie. "That makes me feel a lot better." They got home early enough to prepare a wonderful dinner which they and the girls enjoyed very much. The rest of the evening was full of questions.

"So you found out for sure that her name is Loretta," asked Liana. "Yes," said Robert. "They checked the finger prints on all the belonging they found and they matched. She is really Loretta James. "Tell me about her life," asked Amy. "Where is she from and did you find out anything about her family?"

"We will not know anything until I bring her home," said Robert. "Her home is in Indiana. I will take her home after we get an OK from the Cleveland police."

"Did you find out anything about her family," asked Liana. "We are not sure," said Robert. "Her documents say that she is married to a doctor, but they were not able to locate him. That is all we know. I will fill you all in after I get back from taking her home. Now that is enough. I want to watch a movie on TV."

The next two days went by slowly. Finally he got a call from Sergeant Torino.

"Since he pleaded guilty the judge has not requested a court hearing. He has sentenced him to five years with a possible release after three years with good behavior."

"That is good news," said Robert, "Thank you so much." Then Robert hung up and turned to Lorrie. Robert knew how important it was to Lorrie to go home. "Tomorrow is Tuesday. Pack up all your things and be ready to go home tomorrow." Lorrie jumped with joy.

She didn't hesitate to start packing, although she didn't have too much to pack. The next morning at eight o'clock they were on their way to Indiana. It took them about six hours to get there. As Robert pulled into her driveway the car next door was just ready to pull out. Seeing Robert's car it pulled back into its driveway and a woman got out of the car. As Robert and Lorrie got out of the car she yelled out.

"Lorrie," she yelled, "I'm so happy to see you. How are you? Come here and give me a hug." With that said she walked up to Lorrie and hugged her.

"Do you know me?" asked Lorrie. Before she could annswer

Robert explained all that had occurred since Lorrie left for Ohio.

"I am Melanie Robins, your best friend. Don't you recognize anything about me?"

"All I know is that I like you very much," said Lorrie. "Can you tell me about my husband Ronald?"

"I'm so sorry," said Melanie. "Your husband passed away about two years ago. Look I'm going to take the next week off. We can sit and I will help you recall all of your life. I'm sorry" she added as she looked at Robert. "Who are yoou and how doyou know Lorrie?"

"My name is Lieeutenant Robert Benson. I am the police officer that is in charge of seeing that Lorrie is taken care of. The fellow who hurt her is in jail and Lorrie is home with her friend. So I think I am no longer needed here."

"Why don't you stay here for lunch," said Melanie. "I'm sure you two didn't have anything to eat."

"Thank you very much," said Robert. "But it is a six hour drive. I don't want to get home very late."

"Oh Robbie," said Lorrie. "I guess we are holding you from your next assignment. How can I ever thank you for all that you have done for me?"

"First I hope that you will not forget me," said Robert feeling sad. "I feel that I am more than an assigned officer. I think we are friends." "There will never be a doubt about that," said Lorrie. "Goodbye and God bless you." As Robert walked over to get into his car he heard Melanie ask Lorrie a question.

"Lorrie where is your car? I guess it is at the airport. I think the first thing we have to do is get your car." Lorrie just stood there watching Robert drive away then she turned to Melanie.

"First let's go inside my house," said Lorrie. Robert drove away looking back to see Lorrie perhaps for the last time. As he drove down the street he wondered if he would ever see her again. He had no idea of what the future would bring.

# CHAPTER THREE

# THE NEXT ASSIGNMENT

LORRIE STOOD ON HER front porch as she watched Robert leave. She wondered if she would ever see him again. She wondered why she had such a strong feeling for him.

"Hello Lorrie," said Melanie, "where has your mind gone to now. Are you thinking of the officer that just left?"

"I don't know why I have such strong feeling for him," said Lorrie saying out loud what she was thinking. "Do I care for him because he is the only man I know? Or, do I care for him because he spent so much time taking care of me? Or do I care for him because he is a very sweet and caring man?"

"I think it is because he is a very handsome man," said Melanie. "Anyway let's go inside and see if it refreshes your memory." Lorrie took out the keys in her purse and opened the door. They walked inside.

"What do we do now?" asked Lorrie.

"Well let's walk through the whole house and see how it affects you," said Melanie. They walked through most of the house. "What do you think of what you are seeing?" asked Melanie.

"I just feel like it is familiar," said Lorrie as they entered the small room off the family room.

"This is your office," said Melanie. "I think you should look through all the notes and document here in your desk. I suggest you do it later when you are alone and have the time to do it. Right now we should sit down together and let's review our history."

"Tell me about my husband," said Lorrie. "I don't remember anything about him."

"Later, first let me start from the beginning," said Melanie. "We met at the city hospital. We were both nurses there. After about a year that we met as best friends you left the job to get a master's degree in nursing."

"I have a master's degree in nursing," said Lorrie with a shocked look on her face.

"Yes," said Melanie. "You came back and got a job as the Surgeon's assistance. That is where you met Ronald. He had an office on Market Street. He liked how well you helped him. He said he had gotten too many poor assistants before. He then said that he wanted you to be his personal assistance and office nurse. You then quit your job at the hospital and moved in as his private nurse and secretary. You then assisted all of his surgeries."

"When did we get married?" asked Lorrie. "Did I leave him and go back to the hospital? It didn't seem proper to marry your office assistant"

"Proper or not you were in his office for just about six months," said Melanie, "when he told you that he wanted you not because you were a great surgeon's assistance but because he had fallen in love with you the first time he saw you. You were married the next summer. You continued to work for him until he had his heart attack. You then went back to the hospital but all they had for you was as a common nurse. You were not too happy with that job so you started looking elsewhere."

"Do you know why I went to Ohio?" asked Lorrie.

"I remember that before you came to the hospital you worked for some laboratory that had all kinds of equipment for testing patients. You said that you loved that because you had a chance to evaluate the results of the tests you preformed on the patients. I think there was a place in Ohio that needs someone with your experience in that field of nursing."

"How about you?" asked Lorrie, "how did we meet and tell me about your life? I don't even know if you are married."

"As I said, we met at the city hospital. We worked together. I am married to Bill Robins, who is a corporate manager. His job is to reorganize company plants that are not operating with sufficient profit. He is currently in California to straighten up one of the corporation's largest plant, so that it would provide an adequate profit. "That is enough of our history for now," said Melanie. "Let's go get your car. I'm sure you left it at the Chicago Airport when you left for Ohio" Lorrie did not need to be told twice.

"I agree with that," said Lorrie. She grabbed her keys and they got into Melanie's car. It took about forty minutes to get to the Chicago airport. Melanie parked her car in the airport parking lot and they both got out. "I know that you are too tired from all that you have gone through this day," said Melanie. "So come and have dinner with me. Tomorrow we will have breakfast together and then I will take you to the grocery store where you can buy food you will need for the rest of the week."

"Now what do we do?" asked Lorrie.

"Give me your keys, said Melanie. "I think one of these keys is for your car. Also there is a car location button on the key chain." Lorrie gave her the keys. "Yees here it is," said Melanie said as she pushed the button. At a distance from where they were parked they heard an auto horn sound. They walked toward where they heard the sound. After they walked about a hundred feet Melanie pushed the button again. Again they heard the auto horn sound. This time it was much closer.

"I think it come from a row of cars behind us," said Lorrie. They walked toward the sound.

"There it is," said Melanie. "Isn't that your white Cadillac down this row a short way?"

"I don't know," said Lorrie. "I think it is the one that has its horn blowing. I don't recognize it." When they got to the car, Melanie turned off the horn. She tried the lock button and they heard the lock pop up.

"It is your car," said Melanie. "Get inside and follow me to my car. Then follow me home. Here is a ten dollar bill. You will need it to get out through the parking lot gate. I don't think you have any cash in your purse. You can pay me back when you cash one of your checks." "Thank you," said Lorrie. "I don't have even a penny in cash." After paying the parking fee Lorrie followed Melanie home.

When they got home Lorrie hit the garage door button and the garage opened. She drove her car inside and then came out to meet Melanie. Melanie had also parked her car in her garage.

"Well it is getting near five," said Melanie. "Come over to my house and I'll make us a simple dinner."

"I hate to impose on you," said Lorrie. "You have doone more for me than you have too."

"Look I know that you don't have anything in your refrigerator, I need to buy some food for myself also. Then you can cook and invite me to dinner. We can then take turns cooking dinner. You do one night and I will do the next night. We will do that until one of us has to leave. That could be me. My husband is trying to get a job where he would not have to travel as much. We miss each other. I may just go to California to be with him. Weare just waiting to see how long he needs to stay there to complete the job."

"I hope that you will staylong enough for me to get the feeling of home again," said Lorrie. "Right now I think of Robert's house as my home."

"Come, let's have some dinner at my house," said Melanie. "Then let's go," said Lorrie "I am very hungry." Melanie made a quick spaghetti dinner. After dinner Lorrie left and went directly to bed.

The next morning Lorrie got up took a quick shower got dressed and went down stairs planning to go next door. However before she could get to the door the doorbell rang.

"Who could that be," said Lorrie out loud. She opened the door and there was Melanie.

"Good morning," said Melanie. "I'm glad you are awake. I thought I would bring breakfast to you. I have some scramble eggs and some potatoes. Let's sit down and eat them before they get cold. This other package is hot coffee."

"Wow," said Lorrie. "How am I ever going to make this up to you?" "Make me a fantastic dinner tonight," said Melanie. When they got through eating Melanie took Lorrie shopping. First she drove her around town hoping that it would trigger some memory. They then went to the town's grocery store. Lorrie bought enough food for a whole week. Melanie also bought a few things for herself. They then went home.

"Well I'll leave you to yourself," said Melanie. "I know that you have a million things to do. I will be here about six for a fabulous dinner."

"That will be great," said Lorrie. "I don't know about fabulous but I will do my best." Meanie helped Lorrie bring her food inside before she left. Lorrie started checking all the rooms and all the closets. Next she started looking through all the drawers in the kitchen so that she knew what she had and where everything was. Soon it was eleven thirty. She decided to make herself a couple of sandwiches with the hard salami she had purchasedthat morning. After lunch she decided to look through the office. She kept putting that off because she knew it would bea lot of work. In the office were a filing cabinet, and a large desk which had a large center drawer and three draws on each side of the desk. She decided to start with the filing cabinet for the afternoon. She didn't want to get involved with important information because she had to plan a special dinner for that evening. The filing cabinet she figure had receipts and less important records. That evening Lorrie made Cavatelli with pork neck bones and meat balls. Melanie showed up about five-thirty. Everything was ready at six. They sat down and ate. When finished eating, Melanie took a deep breath.

"I think that was a meal for a king," said Melanie. "I'm mad at you. I can never give you a dinner that even comes close to this."

"Wait until I bring you the dessert," said Lorrie. She then brought out Sicilian Cannoli and coffee.

"Wow," said Melanie, "where did you learn to cook like this?" "I don't know what kind of cook I was before I was taken in by Robert. I learn so much from him and from his daughter. The grandmother was Sicilian born. She taught them some of the Sicilian recipes. I have a few more that I could cook for you."

"You want to embarrass me every other day" said Melanie, "is that it?"

"I can't do this for every meal I cook for you," said Lorrie. "I did this as a onetime only to show you how grateful I am for all that you have done for me."

"Good," said Melanie. "I would not want to feel like a failure every time I eat with you at your house." They both laughed at that last remark.

"You know that I have a lot to do," said Lorrie, but Melanie interrupter her.

"I know that you are going to be very busy going through all of your files," said Melanie. "So why don't we just meet again at my house at six tomorrow."

"Yes," said Lorrie. "I have to go through every folder in the filing cabinet and all that is in the desk. Ialso have to go to the bank and find out how well off I am. I also have to try and locate were I was going in Ohio."

"Well let me know if you need my help," said Melanie. After they sat and discussed some of the past events they had spent together Melanie left.

Lorrie went directly to her office. She pulled out one of the file draws and grabbed a folder. After an hour trying to remember what it was she realized that this was going to take a least a month. Most of the folders were about doctor reports of her visit when she had not felt well. Most of it was before she met her husband. One of the folders was all the receipts of her husband's illnesses. She read them and then threw them in the trash. After reviewing several folders she decided to check the desk drawers next. She could look at the folders in the filling cabinet any time. She was glad she did because in the desk she found her personal phone book. Inside the cover she found a note giving the phone number of the University Hospital in Fairlawn. Before she called she wrote a note listing all that she would tell them, such as how to explain why she didn't show up for the interview and why she didn't call. She then called the number in her phone book.

"University Hospital office, how can I help you?" answered a woman.

"Hi," started Lorrie. "My name is Loretta James. I had an interview,"

"Hi Loretta," she said interrupting her. "I'm so glad that you called. I am Carol. I'm so glad that you are alright. We read all about you in the local paper.

After you called for an appointment, I used my computer to get all the information I could on you. I learned a lot about your credentials. I found that you worked at the Hobart City Hospital. How you also worked as a surgical assistance to Dr. Ronald James. That information is very impressive. I also see that you spent time and have experience in patient, testing equipment such as theX-ray, and all the other testing equipment in the medical testing lab. We would like to hire you. We are going to need an experienced nurse to run our UH Medical Lab. Are you interested?"

"I amextremely interested," said Lorrie. "When do I start?" "Well that is one of the problems," said Carol. "When you didn't show up we hired a student nurse in your place. However Betty, who runs the lab, is retiring this September. We would like to interview you on a day or two before the starting date. I have no doubt that we will hire you. I will send you the actual starting date later."

"That is perfect," said Lorrie. "I have to find a place to live there in Ohio. I also have to sell my house in Indiana. So the timing is perfect." "I will see if any of the people who live in this area are going to sell their homes," said Carol. "I will let you know. When you come here, please bring a copy of your credentials for our records."

"Thank you so much. I will keep in touch," said Lorrie. With that Lorrie hung up. Next she called the real estate office number she had in her phone book

"Hi," she said when someone answered the phone. "My name is Loretta James.

"Hi Lorrie, this is Mary. I wondered when you would call. Are you ready to sell your furniture and house?"

"I think you should come over and let's talk about a decent price." "Dear Lorrie," said Mary. "Don't you remember? I spent half a day going over all your belongings. I even have all the red tags for the furniture you didn't want to keep."

"I was wondering if all that information was still good," said Lorrie, not being completely honest. She didn't remember any of what she said. She did remember seeing a strange sheet in her desk with names a numbers after them.

"They are all fine," said Mary.

"Then come over and let us get started," said Lorrie.

"I have few other things to take care of first," said Mary. "I'll be there in a couple of days." After she hung up Lorrie went to the desk and looked at the sheet with the priceson it.

"It all made sense now," said Lorrie out loud to herself.

She then went back to her desk drawers and went through the files much happier. Going through the files did not bring back a lot of memory but it was like she was reliving the past. Several document puzzled her. In some of the cases she called the number given on the document. Slowly things got cleared up to her satisfaction. It took over a week for her to go through the desk draws and the filing cabinets draws for her to be satisfied with her effort. It was  about then that the phone rang.

"Hello," said Lorrie. "This is Loretta."

"Hi Loretta, this is Carol of the Universal Hospital office. How are you?"

"I'm fine," said Lorrie. "I'm about to sell my house and furniture." "Well I spoke with Betty. She is moving to a larger house. She is currently living in a six room bungalow that she owns. She is thinking of renting it. If you are interested I will have her get in touch with you." "Please do that," said Lorrie. "I do need a place to stay, and a rental is a perfect solution."

"I will have her call you later today," said Carol and hung up. The day went by and no one called. Perhaps, thought Lorrie, that the girl changed her mind. It was about ten the next morning that Lorrie got a call.

"Hi, is this Loretta James?" asked the caller. "Yes this is Loretta, who are you?"

"Hi, I'm Betty Wilson from the University Hospital. I understand that you are interested in renting one of my properties."

"Yes I am," said Lorrie. "I would like to have a few details of the bungalow first."

"I'm sorry to be late in calling you," said Betty. "The reason I am late calling you is that I expected you would want more about the place you wanted to rent. So I made a few pictures and attached them to an E-mail I sent you. Check your computer. Carol gave me your E-mail address."

"Let me look at the pictures andI will call you back," said Lorrie. She then hung up annd went to her computer. She even forgot that she had a computer. She didn't even remember her E-mail address. She looked for an E-mail from Betty. She found it and viewed all the attached pictures. There was a picture of each room and more than one for the kitchen and family room. The bungalow had a kitchen, a living room, a family room, two bath rooms, and two bedrooms. One bedroom was very small, and off the family room was a small room that could be used as a study. Lorrie was very impressed. It was more than she had expected. After reviewing the pictures she called Betty.

"Hi Betty," she said after she was transferred to Betty's phone. "I have reviewed the pictures that you sent me. I am very impressed. It is more than I expected. Why do they call it a bungalow? It is a small house."

"I'm glad you like it," said Betty. "Do you want to rent it?"

"I have one problem," said Lorrie. "I don't know if I can afford it." "Well I understand that you are going to fill my job after I leave," said Betty. "I know what your salary is going to be. It is not that great. So I'll tell you what. I will give you a big discount from what I think I could get. I will not increase it as long as you hold the job at University Hospital." She then told her what the real estate agent told her she could get for the rent of the bungalow. Then she told her what she would ask her for the rent. It was almost forty percent lower that the real estate told her she could get. The rent Betty asked was less than Lorrie had expected.

"That is very reasonable," said Lorrie. "I will like to rent it." "Good," said Betty. "At the bottom of the E-mail I sent you, where my name is written, you will see my address. Please send the rent checks to that address. Call me the day before you are coming up here, to move in. Then I will put the keys in an envelope and put them in the mail box which is located on the wall next to the front door. If you have any question please feel free to call me."

"I will send you two month's rent money right now," said Lorrie. "When you move in stop at the hospital office," said Betty. "You may have a few papers to sign." Theythen hung up. Lorrie then called Melanie.

"Hi Melanie," she said when Melanie answered the phone. "I need some help."

"What do you need?" said Melanie.

"I need two things," said Lorrie. "First I need to rent a good size truck that could haul most of my furniture and stuff. Next I need to hire a strong youth that can help me load the truck here and come to Ohio and help me unload in at my new home."

"Wow, you have purchased a home already?" asked Melanie. "No," said Lorrie. "I have rented a bungalow near where I got a job."

"You got a job too," said Melanie. "That was fast."

"I did that all this afternoon," said Lorrie. "So can you help me with one of those things I need?"

"I can help you get both at the same time," said Melanie. "I have been checking that kind of service myself. I have a friend that I worked with at the hospital. She is older than us and has a son name Jack who is about thirty. He has a large truck and is in the hauling business." She then gave her the name and phone number. Lorrie called immediately.

"Hi," said Lorrie. "Is this Jack?"

"Yes, this is Jack. What can I do for you?"

"My name is Loretta James. I am a neighbor of Melanie Robins." "Yes I know Mrs. Robins," said Jack, "She used to work with my mother. What can I do for you?"

I am going to move to Ohio and I need someone to move most

of my furniture and of course my clothes and other house items. I would like to go as soon as possible. You may have to spend the night there. I will pay for your room and the dinner meal in the evening and of course breakfast in the morning before we come home."

"I can handle that," said Jack "I have a couple of jobs I have to do first. How does Wednesday sound to you?"

"That sounds great," said Lorrie. "That gives me time to pack up some of the stuff."

"I will be there at eight o'clock. I will bring a few boxes in case you run out of the ones you have. I found out that it happens often."

Great," said Lorrie. "See you Wednesday." After she hung up she went into the attic and got all the empty boxes that were there. She then started to pack all the clothes that were in the closet that she wanted to keep. She placed all that she thought were too old to keep in plastic bags. It was a few minutes later that Mary showed up.

"Hi Mary said Lorrie. "I am getting ready to move."

"Good," said Mary. "I think that will leave only the things you want to red flag. What are these in the plastic bags?"

"These are all the clothes that I want to give to charity," said Lorrie.

"Why don't you leave them hanging in one of the near closet," said Mary. "I can red flag them. You can at least get some money for them. What I don't sell I will give them to a charity."

"I never thought of that," said Lorrie. "I will leave that all to you. Here are the keys to the house. I will leave Wednesday morning. You can take over after that." After an hour of packing Lorrie realized that Jack was right. Lorrie ran out of boxes. On Wednesday morning Jack showed up at eight o'clock. He had five large boxes. Lorrie used four of them. Between the two of them they move all the furniture into the truck. They had to remove all the draws out of the furniture so that they could carry it into the truck. One of the dressers had to be taken apart. The last thing they put into the truck was all the boxes. Lorrie placed a blanket and a small folding table in her car in case she needed them to eat since she was taking the kitchen and the main bedroom to Ohio. She took the blanket in case she had to sleep on the floor when she got back and the table so that she could eat when she got back. She placed them in her car so that they would not be sold by Mary at the red flag sale. They finished all the packing and closed the truck doors about ten after ten. Lorrie packed a small lunch for them to eat along the way. She also packed a small suitcase with the things she would need while staying at thehotel. It took them six hours to get to her bungalow. They got there about four in the afternoon. They had eaten the sandwiches at about noon without stopping. They did not want to lose time. It took two hours for the two of them to bring all the furniture and boxes inside and hang all the clothes, set up the kitchen, place all the kitchen equipment including forks and spoons in the kitchen drawers and set up the bedroom furniture. Lorrie wanted everything to be ready so that she could move right in when she got there. They were finished about six and then went to the Hilton Hotel and got two rooms. They then were ready to go out and find a nice restaurant for diner. As they were walking out the door Jack noticed that the hotel had a restaurant right there in the hotel.

"Why don't we just eat here," said Jack. "I don't know about you but I am very tired. I would like to eat and go to bed."

"I agree," said Lorrie. "I think that a hotel of this reputation would have a great restaurant. Let's do it." She was right. They had a fantastic dinner. After dinner they both went to their bedroom. Before they went inside Jack turned to Lorrie.

"What time do you want to get up tomorrow," he asked.

"Let's go down to breakfast at about eight," said Lorrie. "I will meet you there." In the morning they had no trouble getting up. They met at the restaurant. They had a quick breakfast and were on the road by nine. They decided not to stop for lunch. They got home at about three in the afternoon. Luckily Lorrie had a spare key and they went inside. The house was empty. Lorrie had to go into the kitchen to write Jack a check using the kitchen counter to write on.

"Thank you so much for your help," said Lorrie. "I could not have done it without you."

"Thank you for the generous check," said Jack. "I guess this is goodbye. I don't see us meeting again."

"If you ever go to Ohio in one of your jobs," said Lorrie, "please stop in and say hello."

"It's not very likely," said jack, "but I promise to do that. So goodbye, it was so nice knowing you Mrs. James."

"Good bye," said Lorrie. "Have a wonderful life."

"You too," said Jack as he got into his truck and left. Lorrie went inside and checked all the rooms. All the bedrooms were empty. All the closets were empty. Mary had done a great job. As she was looking in the kitchen to see what she had in the refrigerator to eat she noticed a couple of notes on the counter. It was a note from Mary. It reads as follows.

"Dear Lorrie, I have sold almost everything. I was surprised that most of the clothes in the closet were sold for five dollars each. Everything else went in one day. The only thing left is the old couch that has a bad rip in it. We will get together on the money when you get back. Your friend Betty"

With the note was the receipt for the gift to the charity. Lorrie tried to call Melanie but no one was home. Lorrie then went to the car and retrieved the small folding table and the blanket. She set up the small table off the couch. That was where she would have to eat. Fortunately Lorrie had left a couple of spoons and forks and a knife so that she could eat. She had a small dinner from what she had left in the refrigerator. She tried to call Melanie later that evening but there was no answer. That night she curled up on the couch with the blanket and went to sleep. The next day she contacted Mary. In order to finalize everything Mary asked Lorrie to come to her office.

"Hi Mary," said Lorrie as she entered her office. "How are you doing?"

"I'm fine. I was surprised at the results of your red flag sale. Everything you left was sold except a few old torn clothes and the worn out couch. Here is the money I received minus my fee. Lorrie was amazed at the amount of money she received.

"Wow," said Lorrie. "This is so much more than I expected and hoped for. Thank you very much."

"Now since that is over," said Mary, "let's talk about your house. I have an offer that is thirty thousand less than you said was the lowest price you would accept. I would like to get this over with. I have three other houses to take care of. So if I cut my real estate fee in half would you accept this offer?"

"You would cut your fee in half for me?" asked Lorrie.

"You are a very good friend. I would have cut it in half anyway even if you got what you asked for."

"You are a real friend," said Lorrie. "Let's go for it."

"Good I will call them and tell them that their offer was accepted. By the way I had to negotiate with them for an hour to get their final offer."

"When will the sale be complete?" asked Lorrie.

"It should take about two days I would guess," said Mary. "I will call you when all the papers are ready and they have the final check. I think the buyers have to get a loan from the bank."

"That's fine," said Lorrie. "I have several things to do. First I have to go the bank to find out how to transfer my accounts. Then I have to pack the little that I have to get ready to travel." It took two days as Mary had predicted before Mary called. Lorrie quickly went to Mary's office. She signed all the papers and paid Mary the fee she had agreed on. She then got her final check. After saying a sad good bye to Mary, Lorrie went to the bank to deposit the check and also made arrangement for the transfer to the bank in Ohio. That all done she went home to spend the rest of the day. The next morning she got up early and packed all her belonging in her car. She took one last look through the house and got in her car that was in the garage. She had to open the garage door manually because she left the portable garage opener on the kitchen counter. After she pulled the car out she got out to close the garage door manually. She pressed the innside button and had to run out before the garage door closed. As she ran out she saw Melanie's car pull into her drive way. Lorrie walked over to meet Melanie as she got out of her car.

"Melanie," said Lorrie. "Where have you been? I have been trying to call you for a week. Why didn't you answer your cell phone?"

"Hi Lorrie," said Melanie. "How are you? I'm sorry I was in such a hurry that I left my phone in my other purse."

"Why were you is such a hurry?" asked Lorrie. "I hope it was not something bad."

"Come inside and I'll tell you the whole story," said Melanie.

"I can't stay long," said Lorrie. "I have a six hour drive to do today." "Wellcome inside we can at least have a cup of coffee," said Melanie. "Where are you going?" While Melanie was making coffee, Lorrie explained all that had happen.

"I was about to leave for good," said Lorrie, "Thank the Lord that you came home when you did. I own nothing here in Indiana."

"You are breaking my heart," said Melanie. "You see I came home to sell my house and move to California. My husband got a job as the president of the California Company. It is a great job because he will not have to travel so much. I almost felt like I was not married. Anyway the reason I left in a hurry is because Bill has his eye on a beautiful house and he wanted me to see it before he made an offer. He was afraid that it would be sold before I got there."

"I am going to miss you," said Lorrie with tears in her eyes. "You are the only friend that I have." Melanie then hugged her. They both had tears in their eyes.

"I miss you already," said Melanie.

"I better go before we both break down and I will not be able to leave." With that said Lorrie got into her car and pulled out of the driveway. As she was backing up she looked at Melanie who came out and stood sadly watch Lorrie drive off. Lorrie wondered if Robert felt the same way when he back out of the drive leaving her standing there in sadness. The thought caused Lorrie to decide to stop and see Robert when she got to Ohio.

When Robert left the drive way of Lorrie's house in Hobart Indiana, he did look forward and saw Lorrie standing perfectly still watching him leave. It looked like she was very sad at his departure. Robert felt the same way. He wanted to stay but now she had the neighbor Melanie that could run her through the history of her life. He would just be in the way. He left feeling sadder than he had been since Rita passed away. The trip back to Ohio was a very boring trip. He got to his house at about nine that evening. The girls had saved some food for him in the refrigeerator. Robert heated it up in the microwave, ate, and went right to bed.

The next morning he slept in. When he got up the girls had already gone. Robert decided to call Captain Wilson.

"Good morning," said the girl that answered the phone. "How can I help you?"

"Hi Amanda," said Robert. "This is Robert Benson. Please connect me with the Captain." She connected him.

"Hi Captain," said Robert. "I wanted to report back to you about Loretta James."

"Yes," said the Captain, "did you get her home OK and are you still there?"

"No I'm home," said Robert "I returned late last night."

"You didn't leave her alone, in her house," asked the Captain, "which probably was like leaving her nowhere."

"Not at all," said Robert. "She met her neighbor who said she was her best friend. I would not have left her without someone to care for her. Her best friend was a girl named Melanie. She is going to take off a week and take Lorrie through the history of her life. I  left because I thought that I would have been in the way."

"Well, keep in touch with her and me," said the Captain.

"By the way Captain," said Robert. "I want you to remember that I am retired. So I would like it if you will not give me another assignment."

"All right," said the Captain. "Have a good day." With that he hung up. Robert went back to his computer. He wanted to go back to writing his novel. However, his thoughts of Lorrie and how much he missed her kept him from writing. His mind was always around the time he had with her.

The days went by slowly. He found that he could not do much writing on his novel. It was sometime in early August that Amy came to him wanting his attention.

"Daddy," said Amy, "you know that I love you like you were my real father. In fact, I lovve you more than I did my real father and more than most daughters love their father."

"I love you too like my real daughter," said Robert, "however I feel like there is sadness, in there somewhere."

"I just don't want you to think that I could ever forget the love that you have shown me," said Amy.

"All right," said Robert. "What is this all about?"

"I just felt like I should be living in the apartment I have been paying rent these last few months," said Amy. "I think I should go early and try to get a part time job in a nearby hospital. Later when school starts it would be difficult to find a job. I could use the experience."

"Of course you should do what you think is best for your life," said Robert. "You have your whole life to plan. I will miss you very much. I think you are doing the right thing. I hope that you will be able to break away for the holidays. I understand, however, that holidays are probable the days you will be needed most since some of the regular nurses will be taking off. What about your present job?"

"I was just an observer," said Amy, "They would not let me do anything."

"I guess if you got everything you could from them you should leave," agreed Robert.

"Then if it is alright with you I will pack and leave tomorrow morning," said Amy.

"Of course," said Robert. "Is there anything I can do to help you?"
"Just your blessing is all I need," said Amy.

"You have my blessing," said Robert. "I will always pray for your safety, your health, and your success." The next morning as planned Amy packed and was ready to leave.

"I am going to miss you," said Liana as she came for breakfast.

"I know," said Amy. "You are like a sister to me. I am going to miss going to work with you."

"I know," said Liana. "I'm going to feel lonely."

"I have already eaten breakfast," saidAmy. "So I'm ready to leave. I already have my suitcase in the car so good bye to you both." Liana was the first to hug her. Next Roberthugged her.

"Take care now," said Robert. "I hope we will see you for the holidays."

"I love you both so much," said Amy as she when through the door. She got into her car and waved goodbye to Liana and Robert who had followed her out of the house. They waved good bye. Amy sadly left for Cleveland. Robert returned to the house and ate breakfast with Liana. After Liana left for work Robert went into his office to work on his novel.

The days went by very slowly. Robert found it very hard to work on his book. He missed both Amy and Lorrie. Liana began working overtime, so Robert was alone most of the time. It was about two week later, about ten in the morning, while Robert was trying to work on his novel, when someone knocked on his front door. Robert opened the door and there he saw a young woman.

"What can I do for you?" asked Robert.

"Are you Lieutenant Robert Benson?" she asked.

"I'm retired so I am just Robert Benson.," said Robert.

"I know," said the woman. "Captain Wilson told me. He said that perhaps I could beg you and perhaps hire you as my detective to help me."

"That stinker," said Robert. "He figured I could not turn down a woman in trouble. Come on in and let's sit at the table. We can have a cup of coffee while you tell me your story. First of all what is your name."

"My name is Annemarie Casta; Annie is what most people call me. I don't have very much money to hire you with. Our lawyer is rather expensive."

"Let's not worry about that for now," said Robert. "Tell me your problem."

"My husband is in jail charged with a murder that he didn't commit."

"Start from the very beginning," said Robert. "Don't leave anything out."

"It all started whhen I was in high school. I was asked out on a date by a highly popular football player named George Falter. I realize now that I never was in love with him but it was such an honor to be asked on a date with him. After several dates he asked me to be his girlfriend. I was so thrilled. It made me a very popular girl. I said yes. We talked about getting married when he and I were both out of school and had good jobs to support us. He said that I will always belong to him."

"What was he on the team?" asked Robert. "What made him so popular? Was he the quarterback?"

"He was the running back," said Annie. "He was the reason that our team won so many games. All the girls were crazy about him. He was very cocky and confident in himself."

"Well go on," said Robert. "I suspect that you broke up. What caused the break up?"

"He broke it up with me after I graduated. He had graduated the year before me," said Annie. "All of a sudden he stopped calling me. Later I learned that he was dating a TV clothes model. I never heard from him until a few weeks ago. In the mean time I met Johnny and we got married. We have been married over two years when he showed up at our home at about five in the evening. My husband Johnny works in an auto repair shop. He was not home because at this time of the year there is more business that they can handle in just an eight hour day. He works overtime and doesn't usual come home until about eight. We then have supper together."

"How about you?" asked Robert, "What do you do?"

"I am a sales lady at the woman clothing shop. I get off at four- thirty."

"OK then," said Robert, "what did the old boyfriend want from you?"

"He said that I belonged to him and I have been committing

adultery. I should not be sleeping with Johnny. I then told him that I am not his, and that I am married and that I love my husband and if he didn't leave now I will call the police. I then reached for the phone."

"Did he leave then?" asked Roberts.

"He left but he said that it was not over, that I belonged to him and that I would be sorry if I didn't leave the man I was living with."

"Did you call the police?" asked Roberts.

"No," said Annie. "I thought that he would take my answer seriously and I didn't want to cause any more problems. I guess that I should have because two days later at about the same time he came back. When I wouldn't answer the door he kicked it in and grabbed me and almost choked me. He slapped me several times and tried to kiss me. I broke out of his arms and ran outside. After he left, I called the police and they sent out a warrant for his arrest. Of course they could not find him. My husband took the next two days off and was home when I got off from work."

"Did your husband," said Robert, "then go out looking for him?" "No," said Annie. "He stayed home to protect me. It was early in the morning two days later that George showed up. He broke in again,

not worried that my husband was home, perhaps thinking he was at work. Anyway Johnny took out his gun and chased George down towards his car. Johnny yelled that if he showed up again he would kill him. That is when Johnny was distracted by the next door neighbor who yelled out to Johnny to stop making so much noise that early in the morning. When Johnny turned to answer our neighbor, George got the chance to kick the gun out of my husband hand. George being much bigger than Johnny beat my husband up so that he was out for the next thirty minutes. Fortunately he was ok and would not let me take him to the hospital. He didn't want to leave me alone. The next day the police came and arrested Johnny. Johnny was charged with the murder of George Falter."

"What evidence," asked Robert, "did they have against him?" "They found his body in his garage. The pistol that killed him was found next to his body. The pistol was registered to my husband Johnny. Also the neighbor told the police that she saw Johnny pointing a gun at him and threatening to kill him."

"Well weren't you with him from the time he was knocked out by George?"

"No," said Annie, "When I found that Johnny was alright I went to work. We need the money badly."

"Why are you so sure," asked Robert, "that he didn't do it?" "First he is to gentle to do it," said Annie, "and most important is that we are Born Again Christians.

"Well I'll take over from here," said Robert. "I recommend that you call your attorney. Tell him that you have a detective that will investigate the situation and that you will call him back if his service would be needed. If I do what I think I can do for you, you will not need an attorney."

"Thank you," said Annie. "I pray you can be successful and get my husband freed."

"Go home and go back to your regular life," said Robert. "I will contact you if I need anything from you."

The next morning Robert went to the police station. He didn't call Captain Wilson as he usually did when he wanted to see him. Robert walked directly into his office.

"Captain," Robert started. "You are something else. You knew that I could not resist a lady in trouble. So will you assign me to investigate her problem?"

"I can't," said the Captain. "You are no longer a member of this police force. Remember you retired and asked not to be given assignments as a part time member."

"Ok Captain," said Robert, "what is it that you want from me?" "Well I could sign you up again as a part tiime officer, but you have to do something for me."

"All right," said Robert. "What do you need?"

"I need a replacement for you," said the Captain. "You know William Bradman don't you?" "Yes I know Bill," said Robert.

"Bill is a very intelligent man," continued the Captain. "He has a degree in investigative processes. I would like you to take him with you wherever you go and train him as an investigative officer."

"I could do that," said Robert. "What would Bill think of that?" "Well let's ask him," said Captain Wilson as he picked up the phone and asked Bill to come into his office. Bill did not hesitate to come into the Captains office.

"Hi Bobby, said Bill, "How are you?" "I'm fine Bill," said Robert. "Listed Bill," said the Captain, "I have turned over the Case assignment to Robert. Would that offend you?"

"Oh thank the Lord," said Bill. "I was worried that I couldn't handle it."

"I would like you to work with Robert," continued Captain Wilson. He will teach you how to be a great detective."

"I would love that," said Bill. "How do you feel about that Robby?" "I would love the company," said Robert. "I could use your opinion as we do our investigation."

"You guys go do your jobs," said Captain Wilson. With that Bill and Robert left for Bills office.

"Is this your office now?" asked Robert.

"I know," said Bill. "It used to be yours. Remember I am taking your place," said Bill with a large smile on his face.

"Ok," said Robert, "rub it in. let's get to work. Tell me what have you gathered up to now?"

"I found out that George had a girlfriend that was a model. She broke up with him and moved to California. She came back to Ohio to visit a relative and George found out. He went to her and told her that she was his. I don't know what she did that made him so angry that he beat her up and put her into the hospital. He was arrested and spent the next two years in jail."

"So that is why he didn't molest Annie for two years," said Robert remembering what Annie had said to him.

"I understand that he has molested another woman but I don't know who she is," said Bill.

"How about the crime scene," asked Robert, "have you seen it? What is the evidence that has been found there?"

"The body was found in his garage with the murder gun on the floor next to the body," said Bill. "They found that it was registered to John Casta. The responding office said that it was an open and closed case"

"That is one thing you should learn right now." said Robert. "Never accept an open and closed conclusion. Not accepting it will lead you to look for contradictory evidence. If you can't find any at least you looked. You will be amazed at how many times I found contradictory evidence. I believe this case will be a good example.

"I understand what you are saying," said Bill. "I will remember that."

"Did you get a report on the finger prints on the gun?" asked Robert.

"Not yet," said Bill. "Let me check right now." He then went into the lab and brought out the report. "It says here that it was wiped clean."

"Now that is what I am talking about," said Robert. "What idiot would shoot someone with his own gun, wipe it clean and then leave it there."

"I see what you mean," said Bill laughing. "No one would ever be that dumb. What do we do now? Do we go and talk to Annie the wife of the man in jail?"

"No," said Robert "I have already talked to her." Robert then explained all that happened that got him involved. "I think we should go and talk to the wife of the victim."

"Her husband's body has just been released to her," said Bill. "I believe she is busy making arrangements. I will call her cell phone as see if we can make an appointment."

"Go ahead," said Robert. "Since they have released the body I think the autopsy is complete. I'll see what it says." When Robert returned with the autopsy report bill had just gotten off the phone.

"I contacted Vera Falter," said Bill. "She gave me a hard time at first. She didn't see whhy we wanted to continue the investigation. I told her that it was just routine duty before we close the investigation. I told her that it would probably not change anything. However, even if the chance of us finding anything is small, don't you want to be absolutely sure we have the right man who murdered your husband? Anyway she gave in and we have an appointment with her at four tomorrow evening. That is after the funeral burial activity."

"That is great," said Robert. "I have here the doctor's obituary report. It says that he died from a bullet wound to his chest. However at the bottom of the report is something strange. He found that he had some bloody skin under his finger nails that was not his. Neither the skin nor the blood is his. They also found several bruises on his face and shoulders. I think that before he was shot he had a struggle with his assailant."

"I guess we have to look for someone with bruises and a scratch on his body," said Bill.

"Why don't you get a list of all the members of George's family," said Robert. "I will see what I can find out about the model that he sent to the hospital."

"I will get right on it," said Bill. Robert then left the office and went to the front office. Robert got on the front office phone and called the North Canton police department.

"Hello, this is Corporal Rick Brown, how can I help you?"

"I'm Lieutenant Robert Benson of the Fairlawn Police. I'm calling to ask you about the model that was beaten by George Falter."

"Yes I head of the murder that took place in Fairlawn," said Rick. "It was a good deed for the world. Anyway the girl that was mistreated was called Lilly Lane. Just a minute and I will pull her record." A few minutes later Rick came back to the phone. "Her real name was Lillian Corvellio the record show that she originally left for California to get away from George. She stated that he toldher that she belonged to him and she had to make it official. She didn't even like him she said. She only came back a month ago because of her mother's serious illness. She tried to keep it secret, but a slick news reporter found out and wrote an article on her return. That is when George found out about it and came to reclaim Lilly. I think she hit him to escape from him. That is when he beat her up and sent her to the hospital. George was charged with assault and battery and given two years in prison."

"Does she have any relatives in this area?" asked Robert.

"No," said Rick. "Her mother was the only relative and she has since past away. After the burial, Lilly went back to California. We did do a complete search for other relatives or close friend and found none." "Thank you very much," said Robert. "Would you please send me a copy of her record?"

"I will be glad to," said Rick. After that they both hung up. Robert then went looking for Bill.

"Hi Bill," said Robert after he found Bill in his office. "What have you found out?"

Well first of all, the one I checked is George's wife," stated Bill. "Her name is Vera. She is the one we have an appointment with at four this afternoon. She has a sister named Helen, who is married to a man named Vincent. Next I checked George's family. He has a sister named Sophia. He had a mother names Martha and a father named Joseph."

"I guess soon or later we will have to talk to all of them," said Robert. "Right now let's get ready to visit Vera. First let's go to lunch." "I brought my lunch," said Bill. He then opened his desk drawer and pulled out a bag.

"I'll see you later then," said Robert as he walked out of the office.

That afternoon about five minutes to four thhey arrived at Vera's house.

"Come on in," said Vera when they arrived at her front door. Apparently she was waiting for them. "I really don't understand why you want to do this."

"It is only a formality," said Robert. "We will not take up much of your time."

"Well I did my duty," said Vera. "I took care of his burial. As you can figure out I was no longer in love with him. He was not a good husband. He cheated on me more than you can number."

"Why did you stay with him?" asked Bill.

"First of all I am a Christian," said Vera. "I think the Lord gave me the job to try to save him. Secondly I threatened him once. I said that if he didn't stop molesting other woman I would divorce him. I thought he was going to kill me. He told me that I belonged to him and the only way I was going to get out of this marriage was to die. So from then on I kept silent on the subject. I only tried to warn him that the Lord was against what he was doing. He told me several times that if Solomon of the Bible could have more than one wife so could he."

"Didn't you have him checked for his mental state?" asked Bill.

"I took him once to a special doctor," said Vera. "I told him to come with me, that I was taking him some place special. I tricked him into thinking the tests they were going to give him would surprise him in a special wonderful feeling. The test, the doctor told me proved that he was a conceded, selfish, cold hearted man, who had an erroneous interpolation of the bible. However, he said, there was not enough evidence to declare him insane and place him into an institution. After the test I told him that I was sorry but the system didn't work with him."

"Are there any other women, who you were aware of, that your husband could have molested?" asked Robert.

"I'm sure there were, but none that I know of," said Vera.

"Well Mrs. Falter," said Robert. "Thank you so much for your time. We hope that you will be well."

"I am better without George," said Vera as Robert and Bill stated to leave. "By the way, you may be interested to know that they asked me to testify against Mr. Casta and I refused. If he did it I don't blame him with all the harassment my husband gave him and his wife."

"Thank you," said Robert as they left.

"That was the weirdest investigative conversation I ever was involved with," said Bill.

"It is understanddable," said Robert.

"What are our next moves in this investigation?" asked Bill

"I think you should find out all you can about George's family. Check what you can find about his mother, father, and his siblings."

"I can do that," said Bill. "I will get right on it. What are you going to do? Do you want to meet later today?"

"I think I should investigate any members of Vera's family. I'm sure that all members of her family were unhappy at the way George treated Vera. I will take on that job. However, it is getting late. Why don't we meet tomorrow morning and discuss what each of us has found." When they got back to the office Robert dropped Bill off and went home. Bill went directly into his office and did research on George's family. After some phone calls and research from the city records he looked for the phone numbers for his father Joseph, his mother Martha and the phone for his a sister Sophia. They all had the same number. Using the phone number he got, he called, hoping they were all available. It was almost five. They all had to be home.

"Hello,' said a woman's voice. "Who is this?"

"Hi, my name is William Bradman. I am a detective with the Fairlawn Police department. I am investigating the death of George Falter. I believe you are his mother. I would like to ask you a couple of questions. These are just routine question that are necessary to close the case."

"I think you should ask my daughter these questions," said Martha, George's mother. "She is more knowledgeable of George's activities."

"May I speak to her then please?" said Bill.

"Hi," said voice that suddenly came on the phone. "My name is Sophia. I am George's sister. What is it that you want to know?"

"Well as you know George was killed a few days ago," started Bill. "I was wondering if you know of anyone else who would have wanted to see him dead."

"I see that there is something that you are not aware of," started Sophia. "We have not seen or talked with George for over eight years. Let me tell you about George's history here at home. About eight years ago George and my mother had a disagreement. I think it was about money. Hewanted to buy something and my mother said no. All this is not important to you so I will not load you with the details. What is important is that George got so angry that he slapped my mother in the face and then punched her shoulder as she turned away from him. My father grabbed him and threw him outside. He told him that he was lucky that they were not back in the days of Moses. In those days they stoned a disrespecting son. So he just told him to never come anywhere in the city. George left and has never been seen since. So you see we could not help you in any way."

"I understand," said Bill. "I'm very sorry that I disturbed you." That said he hung up the phone and went home.

In the meantime Robert was getting all the information he could on Vera's family. He found out that Vincent had been arrested for being in a bar fight. He thought that made him a good suspect. Next he checked Helen's record. She had no record. He then called Helen.

"Hello," said Helen as she answered the phone. "This is Helen." "Hello Helen," said Robert. "My name is Robert Benson. I'm a detective with the Fairlawn Police Department. It is required that we talk to all members of the victim's family. I would like to come over and talk with you. It shouldn't take but a few minutes." "Is this necessary?" asked Helen.

"I'm sorry," said Robert. "It is the law."

"Ok," said Helen, "come tomorrow night about five?"

"That's fine," said Robert "See you then." Robert then hung up. He left himself a note and went home. The next day Robert met Bill at the police station.

"Good morning Bill. How are you today?"

"I'm fine," said Bill. "What are our plans for today?"

"First tell me what you found out about George's family," said Robert.

"Well there is not much to tell," started Bill. "It seems like George had a fight with his mother. Somehow in the fit of anger he stuck his mother first with a slaap in the face and then a punch on her arm. His father threw him out of the house and threatened that if he should even step into the city he would regret it. They haven't seen or heard from him in about eight years."

"I guess that is a dead end," said Robert. "I got an appointment with Helen, George's sister in law. She is Vera's sister. The appointment is for five tonight. I'll pick you up at four-thirty here at your office. Until then I have some shopping to do. See you then." Robert then left to go and buy some groceries he needed to eat supper that night.

At exactly four-thirty Robert arrived at Bill's office. They both then went to Helen's house. Helen had expected them and opened the door as they stepped on the front porch.

"Come on in," said Helen. "I don't know what I can do for you. I really don't think this is necessary."

"I know," said Robert as he came in the door. "It is the law. We have to interrogate all who knew George."

"Well before we start come on in and sit at the kitchen table. I have made some coffee." She then poured a cup of coffee for the three of them. "Well where do we start?" asked Helen.

"First of all," started Robert. "Tell us the details of when George first abusively molested you." Robert didn't know if George even met her. He decided to pretend to know that George had molested her. He wanted to see how she would deny it. As it turned out she didn't deny it.

"How did you find out about that?" asked Helen feeling betrayed. "Information like that gets around," said Robert. "We don't remember who told us and if we did we could not tell you."

"Well he came here and told me that when he married my sister he also married me," said Helen. "He said that I belonged to him."

"What did you do?" asked bill.

"I tried to push him out the door," related Helen. "He grabbed me by the arm and slapped me. He told me that I belonged to him and should obey him. H tried to kiss me. I screamed and fortunately my neighbor heard me and yelledback that she was going to call the police. George then immediately left."

"Did the neighbor call the police?" asked Robert knowing that she had not.

"No I asked her not to," said Helen. "I didn't want to start a problem and most of all I did not want my husband to know. My husband is worse than George. My husband is very arrogant and quick to react to his anger. Besides, I really believed that George would not come back."

"He did come back didn't he," said Robert.

"Yes he did come back two days later, admitted Helen. "My husband had found out about it from my neighbor. He took the next two days off. So he was home when George came. My husband came out when I open the door and pointed his rife at him. My husband told him that if he came again he would shoot him drag him inside, call the police and tell them that he broke into the house and tried to rob us" Just then Helen's husband Vincent came home from work.

"What is going on?" he asked.

"I am detective Robert Benson. This is just a routine check of all who knew George Falter," said Robert. Then changing the subject he asked him a question. "How did you hurt your neck? It looks like you have a bad scratch on your neck. It looks like it is infected."

"I was trying to trim my tree and a branch caught me as I tried to come down," said Vincent.

"You know that at the police academy police take a course in medical Aid. We needed it because most of the time when there is an accident or some injury it is the police that arrive at the scene first. Many times it is the police that call the ambulance. Therefore it is necessary that we have to be able to provide medical aid."

"That is great," said Vincent. "But why are you telling me?" "I'm telling you because I think you need help and I could provide it," said Robert. "I see you have a cut on your neck and it looks like it is infected."

"I know," said Vincent, "it kindof burns. Can you help me?" "Of course," said Robert.Then he turned to Bill. "Bill, go out to my car. Here are the keys. Bring me my First Aid Kit that is in the trunk." A few minutes later Bill came in with the First Aid Kit. Robert removed the bandage that was poorly attached to his neck. Robert had suspected that Vincent was the killer of George. There was no one else that it could have been thought Robert. So he placed the old bandage in the plastic bag that the new sterile pads came in. He noticed that there was blood on the bandage and that some skin came off with the old bandage. He cleaned the wound and covered it with disinfecting iodine. He then placed the pads on the wound and fastened it with water proof bandages.

"There," said Robert, "that should heal it in a couple of days." "Thank you," said Vincent. "So what can I do for you?"

"I just wondered what you knew about George."

"All I know," said Vincent, "is that he molested my wife. I threatened him with my rifle and he never came back. That was the last time I saw him."

"Well that is all I need to know," said Robert. "I just needed to say that I interviewed all that knew George. So Bill and I will leave now. Thank you for your time and have a great day." After Bill said goodbye they both left. Robert then brought the bandage to the police lab. He asked them to compare the blood and skin with the ones found under George's finger nails. He then went home. The next morning when he went to the police station he was met by Captain Wilson.

"Hi Robert," said the captain. "You did a wonderfful job. The blood and skin matched. I have sent a couple of police to arrest Vincent Brandon for the murder of George Falter."

The next day they brought Vincent to the city court. Robert was asked to testify.

"We have proof that you killed George Falter," said Judge Radcliff. "Now you can get your own lawyer or the court can appoint one for you. However it will be much easier for you if you tell us what happened." Vincent hesitated for a while than decided to confess.

"I just went over there to tell him to stay away from my wife. I threatened him and he started a fight. After he saw that he could not beat me he went to the table he had in the garage and grabbed his gun. I don't know why he had a gun in his garage. It was his gun not my gun. He was ready to shoot me. I tried to take the gun away from him and in the struggle the gun went off. I had twisted his arm so the gun was pointed to his chest. I should have left the gun alone.

I think the only finger print on the gun were his. I however I wiped the gun, and thinking it was his, I left it there and left."

"Do you have anything to add," said the Judge to Robert.

"The gun was taken from Mr. Casta when they struggled at Mr. Casta's home. The wound in Mr. Falter's chest did show signs of gun powder and the bullet entered at an angle."

"I will have to take all the information," said the judge, "review it to consider whether it is can be called an accidental death. Court dismissed." Robert then went back to the Captain's office.

"Well Captain," said Robert. "Am I needed anymore?"

"No," said the Captain. "You have done a fantastic job. I don't believe you will be needed any more. You can go and have a wonderful retirement." Robert got into his car and started to go home. He should have felt relieved however he found that he was very sad. The job had taken his mind off of Lorrie. Now all he could think about was Lorrie. Would he ever see her again?

CHAPTER FOUR

# THE LONG AND LONELY DAYS

THE DAYS WENT BY very slowly. Robert felt all alone. His girls were all in school. He tried to continue writing his book but he found that it was difficult to concentrate. He did finish his first murder story but he got an Author Memory Block as they called it. It was two days later when he decided that he would rest from writing. He decided since it was around five and the weather had turned nice and warm for September, he decided to pull his grill out of his garage. The garage doors are at the rear of the house. So all he had to do is pull it out onto the cement area behind his garage. He then turned it on. His plan was to cook some lamb chops on the grill and eat them on the picnic table he had in his back porch. The door to his porch was on the right of the garage cement area. The porch had large windows on two sides. The windows opened like awnings. The picnic table was usually in the rear of the lot under the trees. It was place in the porch in the winter to protect it. However since his wife Rita passed away he kept the picnic table in the porch. That was where he was going to eat his lamb chops that evening. He was waiting for the grill to worm up when a car pulled in the drive way in the rear of the lot next to where Robert was. A woman got out of the car. Robert recognized her.

"Annie," said Robert. "How are you? What are you doing here?" "I came to thank the gentleman who saved my life." said Annie. "How did I save your life?" asked Robert.

"You saved my husband who is my life," said Annie as she came up to Robert and hugged him.

"I was just doing my job," said Robert.

"We love you," said Annie. "You are like a family member to us." "Where is your husband?" asked Robert changing the subject. "My husband is at work," said Annie. They got way behind while he was in jail. He is an auto mechanic as you know. The cars that needed work have stacked up more than they could handle in a forty hour week. He will work twelve hour a days and will probable work on Sunday. Anyway the reason I came by is to tell you that we didn't forget you. We want to be like family. When things get settled we want to invite you to dinner at our house. I will cook you a meal you will never forget. I am Italian and my mother taught me how to cook Cavatelli with pork neck bones and her special meat balls."

"I can hardly wait," said Robert. "How about having dinner with me tonight? I am about to grill some Lamb chops. I have enough for two."

"I'm sorry," said Annie, "I have to go home and cook for John. He will be home about eight. He will be very hungry. So I have to go home. I will call you when things settle down and John will be home at about four-thirty. Whhen that happens I will invite you to dinner. For now I will say good bye." She then wrapped her arms around Robert and kissed him on both cheeks.

It so happened, after all was settled in Indiana, that Lorrie started to drive to her new home. On the way she decided to visit Robert. When she got to Robert house she went to the front door. When no one answered she started to walk to the backyard thinking that Robert, on such a nice day, might be there. As fate would have it she walked to the end of the building and saw Annie hugging and kissing Robert. She thought that her heart would break. She had never felt such a sadness that she could remember. She never even believed that it would be so hard to loose someone. She wondered if this was the way she felt when her husband passed away. She finally got to her new house. She was amazed that she got there safely. She was blinded with tears all the way. She went to bed crying her way to bed.

Back at Robert's house Robert said goodbye and Annie left. Robert felt a little better due to Annie's visit. He felt like he was not alone. His two young girls were far away and he wouldn't see them any time soon. He would see Annie and John soon. He had no idea that Lorrie had been there. He ate his lamb chops and spent the rest of the evening watching a mystery movie on his television. Soon he went to bed. He went to sleep thinking of Lorrie.

The days went by slowly. It soon was Thanksgiving Day. Robert's mother invited him for thanksgiving dinner. Tommy and Liana also came to the diner. Amy had to work. They all enjoyed being together.

The next day Robert went to work on his noveol. He felt a little more encouraged. Time went by and it soon was Christmas. Robert's mother invited them all to dinner at her place. She had told all the kids that they could have holidays any place they wanted but Christmas was always going to be at her house. This time they all came to the dinner. Amy found a way to get away from the part time work at the hospital. Robert's mother had a beautifully cooked turkey. After enjoying a great dinner they exchanged gifts. They all enjoyed being together. Robert was happy to be with them all but he still missed Lorrie. He remembered when Lorrie had been there  after their trip to the Cleveland Zoo. He missed her so much. New Year's Robert spent alone.

It was in the early spring. Robert was having an author's block on writing his novel. He had just decided to give up working on his novel for the day that he got an emergency call from Captain Wilson.

"Robert," started the Captain. "I know that you are retired and that I promised to not assign you to another case. But this is an emergency. It is a double murder and I assigned it to Bill. He needs your help very badly." Robert was getting ready to cook his dinner but decided to put dinner off for a while.

"All right," said Robert. "Give me the address and I'll go right now." The Captain gave him the address and Robert left immediately. When he got there, the police who had closed the area recognized Robert and let him in. Bill had just arrived a few minutes before Robert "Hi Bill," said Robert "I see that it is a woman and a man who have been shot."

"Yes," said Bill, "the neighbor who called us said that it was the husband and wife that she was worried about. She said that she would come over if we needed some information. She did not know that they had been shot. She only heard gun shots. It looks like the husband shot his wife and then shot himself.

"We will have to talk to the neighbor later," said Robert. "Remember what I taught you about what looked like open and closed cases." Robert then walked up to the woman. He felt her head. "She had been dead for about an hour." He then walked up to the man. He felt his head. "He died a few minutes ago. Also if this is his house look at the mess there is in this room. It looks like someone was looking for something very badly. I also notice that the rooms I passed getting here to the bedroom are also very badly messed up. Why would the owner of the home have to do this kind of a searching?"

"I wonder what soomeone was looking for," said Bill. Robert then took out his pen and a magnifier unit from his briefcase. He placed the pen in the barrel of the gun and lifting it up checking it with the spy glass for fingerprints.

"Bill," said Robert. "Do you think that this fellow wiped the gun clean before he shot himself or after he shot himself?"

"Very funny," said Bill with a smile on his face. "I guess there has to be someone else involved."

"I think we should go next door and talk to the neighbor," said Robert. "In the meantime let the doctors take the bodies to the lab and do an autopsy. I noticed that the woman has some bruises on her face and body. Anything they can find my help us."

"Let's go next door," said Bill. "I don't think it would be great for her to come here and see her neighbors in this condition. Let's see what she has to say."

"Do you think she is home this early in the day?" asked Robert. "When I got here I noticed that her garage door was open and her car was in the garage." Robert and Bill then went next door. They knocked on the door and a young lady opened the door. "Come on in, she said. "How can I help you?"

"My name is William Bradman," said Bill, "and this is Robert Bensen. We are Fairlawn police detectives. I am surprised to see you home. Don't you have a job?"

"My name is Phyllis Carson. I only work three days a week. I had yesterday and today off. I guess you want to know why I called you. But first tell me that Dolores and Philip are ok."

"I'm sorry," said Bill. "They are both gone. They have both been shot." Robert and Bill saw tears coming out of Phyllis's eyes.

"She was my best friend," said Phyllis barely getting the words out. Robert and Bill let her rest for a while to let her get settled. Then Robert spoke.

"Tell us all that you know about this problem," asked Robert. "Please start from the beginning. First tell us their full name"

"Their full names are Philip and Dolores Bladen. It was about two days ago," started Phyllis. "She came here crying. She told me that she and Phil had a fight. It was about money. The fight that was about something Phil wanted to buy. She accused him of marrying her for her money. That's when Phil said he was going to divorce her."

"Well if they got divorced would he get half of the money anyway?" asked Bill.

"I think they had both signed an agreement that if they got a divorce he would get nothing. He answered saying that a divorce will prove he didn't marry her for her money. Anyway this morning a little after noon I thought I hear a gun shot. There was silence after that so I ignored it. I thought maybe it was a car's backfire. I wanted to call Dolores but I noticed that there was a black car in her drive way and I realized she had a visitor, so I didn't call. I also saw Phil's car come in the drive about four-thirty so I thought that everything was going to be alright. Then I hear another gun shot. That is when I tried to call Dolores. When she didn't answer is when I decided to call the police. I wish I had called Dolores this morning. At least then I might have saved Phil's life."

"What happened with the black car that you saw here earlier," asked Bill. "Can you describe it to us?"

"It was a small old black foreign car," said Phyllis. "I don't know more than that."

"Did Phil's car come up behind the black car," asked Robert.

"Yes," said Phyllis wondering why Robert asked thhe question. Why do you ask," she finally asked.

"Well if the suspect left before the police got here and with the house on one side and the fence on the other side the suspect had to remove Phil's car to leave."

"Can you tell us if you know any of Dolores's or Philip's family?" asked Bill.

"I know that Dolores had a cousin that she loved like a sister," said Phyllis. "I think that her name was Sylvia. I don't know her last name." "I think that we have enough information to work on," said Robert. "Thank you so much for yourinformation. If we need anything else we will call you."

"You are welcome," said Phyllis. "Please let me know when the funeral will be. I want to attend to say my last goodbye." Robert and Bill then left. On the way to each of their cars, Bill turned to Robert.

It looks like someone tried to get something from Dolores and killed her when she would not co-operate," started Bill. "He then searched on his own to find it. Phil then happened to come home at the wrong time and was killed to keep him silent."

"That sounds like a good analysis," said Robert. "I think he was looking for the agreement that they sign that would eliminate Philip from a share in their wealth. He also was probably looking for the last will and testament of each."

"That is funny," said Bill. "We didn't find any of those documents." "Either we just didn't find them yet or the killer did find them," said Robert."

"Where do we go from here?" asked Bill.

"First of all, make sure that we get some one here to check for finger prints on everything, all the drawers, the door knobs, and including Phil's car," said Robert. "Next I think that we should divide the tasks that we need to do. You check out Dolores's family and I will check out Philip's family. Right now I am going to the grocery store. I don't think I have any food for the rest of the week." They both got into their cars and left. Robert went directly to Giant Eagle grocery store. While he was looking through the vegetable countere he noticed a woman across the counter. He was shocked. doing here? I thought you were still in Indiana."

"I sold everything in Indiana and moved here," said Lorrie in an unfriendly voice. She then started to leave.

"Why haven't you called me?" asked Robert. "I tried to call you but it said that the phone was no long active."

"Look Robert," said Lorrie in a very disturbed attitude. "I have my life and you have yours. Goodbye it was nice knowing you." She started to walk away.

"Lorrie," said Robert in a very disturbed voice. "What is wrong? Did I do something wrong. Are you angry that I left you in Indiana? I thought you agreed with my leaving." Lorrie didn't answer and walked up to the checkout counter. She had her money ready and left before Robert could say anything more. Robert then continued with his shopping. He was very upset with the whole affair. He went home after finishing with his shopping but he was too upset to eat. That night he went to bed but he didn't sleep a wink.

The next day he decided that they didn't check out the house as thoroughly as they should have. He went to the house and let himself in. As he walked into the living room he decided to start there. He didn't expect to find anything there but he thought he had to do it to be thorough. He looked under every pillow and every corner of the room. Then he did the same thing in the kitchen and the dining room. He next went into the bedrooms. He found nothing there. He finally went into the study. He felt that if the documents were anywhere they should be there. He searched through each folder in the filing cabinet. He found a personal phone book. He looked through the book to see if he recognized any of the names. At the end of the book he found strange instructions. It was turn left to 30 turn right past 30 to 12 and back to 0. Robert looked for a combination lock but didn't find one. He then continued on with his search. He searched through every book on the book shelf. He went through the desk checking every item in it. He found no trace of the document. He was about to leave when he remembered a movie he had seen where in the movie they found the document they searched for behind a picture on the wall. Robert then decided to study. That is where he thought would be the best place to put a document. Few people would enter into a man's private office. There was a large picture hanging over a table that was on the opposite wall from the desk. He pulled the picture awayfrom the wall to look behind it. He was shocked at what he saw. Behind the picture was a wall safe. He remembered that in the preliminary search that he did when he first got there that the personal phone book had strange instructions like the instruction to open a lock. He went to the desk and found the personal phone book. He went to the last page and found the information he was looking for. He used to combination instructions and found that it opened the safe. In the safe besides some money he found a last will and testament for each and the signed agreement. He took the documents and went to the police office. He showed them to the Captain and to Bill.

"We may need these later," said Robert. "The wills both say that if either one died that the other would inherit all. The signed document says that if they divorce that Phil would get nothing." He then placed the document in the police safe.

"I am going to find Dolores's family," said Bill. "Have you started to look into Phil's family?" Bill asked Robert.

"No,' said Robert. "I have been busy looking for the documents. I'm going home to start my investigation. I can do it better from there." With that said Robert left for home. Bill went to his computer to see who he could fine that was related to Dolores. He found that she had only one relative. It was a cousin named Sylvia Howe. He looked up her phone number and decided to call her first. If he couldn't get her on her phone, he would check her work place. He knew that as a last resort he may have to go to Cleveland to find her. He dialed her home number. No one answered. He was about to search for her work number when Vicky walked into his office.

"Bill," she said, "You have a visitor."

"Let her in," said Bill. At that Vicky led in a young high class looking woman in the office.

"Hi," she said," Are you Officer Bradman?"

"Yes," said Bill wondering what this young lady wanted.

"Hi, she started, "I went to see my best friend and the place was surrounded by police. When I asked what happened they told me to see you. What is going on? Are they sick with a contagious disease?"

"My lord," said Biill. "Are you her cousin Sylvia Howe?" "Yes, did she ask for me?" asked Sylvia.

"Oh Sylvia, I'm so sorry," started Bill, "Please come in and sit down. I have very bad news for you. Both Dolores and Phil are no longer with us." Bill had not finished his sentence when Sylvia started to cry. She turned around in her chair so that she was not in Bills direct sight. She cried for at least fifteen minutes. Bill was ready to call for help when she turned around and asked Bill the only question she had in mind.

"What happened?" she asked.

"They were both shot by an intruder," said Bill. She was very silent for a while. Bill then broke the silence. "May I get you a cup of coffee of something?"

"No thank you," said Sylvia after a while, trying to recover from the shock. "I knew something was wrong but I never thought it was this bad. What happened?"

"That is what we are trying to find out," said Bill.

"The first thing I would like to know is how you fit into their family." "I am her cousin," said Sylvia. "We were like sisters. I loved her very much."

"The first information we got is that they had a fight over money. What do you know about that? Do you know about their financial problems?"

"They did have a problem about their money," said Sylvia. "They always fought over it. Dolores always accused Phil that he married her for her money. She could never get over that. However, Phil was the nicest guy. He really loved her. The proof of his love is that he took a lot of bull from her."

"What do you know about her money?" asked Bill

"Dolores's father was one of three brothers," started Sylvia. "One was my father and Uncle Fred was the oldest of the brothers. He was a great investor. He worked for a company that designed the first cell phone. He invested everything he had in that company, He finally sold out and invested in thhree othercompanies he helped grow. The thing is that when he died he left over six million dollars which was split between me and Dolores. We each got three million dollars."

"Can you think of anyone who hated them enough to kill them?" asked Bill, "maybe someone who wants to inherit the money?"

"I can't think of anyone in my family or Dolores's family," said Sylvia. "I don't know anything about Phil's family. They all live in Pennsylvania."

"Are you going to apply for some of Sylvia's money?" asked Bill." "Absolutely not," said Sylvia. "My three million has grown to over four million. I don't need more nor do I want more. Let Phil's family inherit all of her and his money."

"That is very kind of you," said Bill. "Unless you have something else to add you may leave."

Robert was deep in his computer trying to find out all he could about Philip's family. He remembered that in his will he left everything to his two sisters who both lived in Pittsburg Pennsylvania. The first is named Natalie Lopez. Her husband is Anthony. In his investigation he found out that they had two children, a boy and a girl. Both are living in western states and will not be available for their funeral. The second is named Carmela Sherman. He found out that she is a widow. She has one son named Benjamin who lives with her. Robert was surprised that in Dolores's will she never said a word about what she wantaed if both died, while  in Phil's will he listed his sisters if they both died. He tried to call each separately but no one answered. He suspected that this early in the day that both families were at work. Robert then went to the police station. He went into Bills office.

"Hi Bill," said Robert. "How are you coming in investigating into Dolores's family?"

"I'm all finished," saidBill with a smile on his face. "I have interviewed her cousin Sylvia and gotall the information I need. She came into my office. I didn't have to go looking for her."

"That is great," said Robert. "What did you find out?"

"She told me that there were three brothers. One was her father another was Dolores's father and the third, the oldest was their Uncle Fred who was never married and had no other relatives. He invested and worked for a company that built and designed cell phones. The important fact is that when he died he left three million dollars to both Dolores and Sylvia. Sylvia said she wants no part of their money. She said to give it all to Phil's family"

"I can see where they would have problems with money," said Robert. "I think that from what you have uncovered the whole investigation is going to center on Phil's family. In my investigation I have not found any other members of Phil's family besides the two sisters and their families. I am going to call them tonight and inform them of the death of their brother and see where that leads me."

"Well I don't see what more I can do at this time," said Bill. "Remember," said Robert, "that this is your assignment. I am only an assistant."

"Ya sure," said Bill with a questioning smile on his face. "Then assist me and tell me what we should do next."

"Let's wait until I contact them," said Robert. "Then you can take over from there." They both left with a smile on their faces.

Robert went to Giant Eagle. He needed some bread and a bottle of milk. As he walked in he saw Lorrie at the checkout counter.

"Hi Lorrie," said Robert with a loving smile on his face. To his surprise and painful feeling she just turned her head and didn't answer. Before Robert could survive from the shock she was gone. Robert got what he went there for paid for them and went home. It was near diner time when he settled down enough to remember that he had a phone call to make. He made the call. A woman answered

"Hello," she said.

"Hello," said Robert. "TThis is Robert Bensen. I am with the Fairlawn Ohio police force. I am calling to speak with Natalie Lopez."

"I am Natalie Lopez," she answered. "What can I do for you?" "Hi Natalie," saaid Robert. "I am calling to give you bad news.

Your brother Philip Bladen and his wife were both murdered. I would like to talk to you if you come to the funeral." There was silence for a while then she answered.

"What do you want to know?" she asked. "We were not very close. It wasn't Phil that kept us apart. Phil was a very kind and loving person. It was Dolores that was the problem. She looked down on us as if we were nobody. She was the high class and we were the low class." "If you don't want to talk now I would understand. I imagine you are very sad," said Robert.

"No, it is alright," said Natalie. "I don't mind answering your questions. We could talk more when I come to Ohio."

"When was the last time you were in touch with your brother?" asked Robert.

"I was not personally in touch with him, but we sent a messenger to talk him into helping us."

"What kind of help do you need?" asked Robert.

"It was more for my sister Carmela," said Natalie. "Her husband got a bad case of cancer. She took him to Chicago at the cancer center there. She mortgaged her house and sold some furniture in a garage sale and she put everything she had to try and save him. It didn't work. Carmela is on the verge of losing everything she has. We know that my brother would do anything to help us. We heard that his wife had a lot of money. She would not let Phil sent any of it to us."

"That may explain the fight that they had before they were shot," said Rodger. "What means did you use to request money from Phil?" asked Robert.

"Carmela sent her son Benjamin to ask him for help," said Natalie. "It didn't work. All that Bennie could get was one thousand five hundred dollars. It was all from Phil's savings."

"I think that explains the fight they had," said Robert. "I don't know if you heard but they had separated. Dolores accused him of marrying her for her mooney. He said adivorce will prove he didn't want her money. It was wheen he went back for something that he was killed. He was shot about an hour after she was shot."

"Oh my," said Natalie. "I didn't know that Dolores was killed also. Who would do such a thing?"

"That is what we are trying to find out," said Robert. "Do you know of anyone who would do such a thing," asked Robert as a final question.

"No I don't know of anyone," said Natalie. "At least no one in my family would do such a thing. You know that we are Born-again-Christians. We let God take care of things like this."

"Thank you so much for your time and information. If you think of anything else tell me when you come to the funeral. Now I need to call your sister."

"I'm afraid she will not be home at this time. She works for a restaurant and is on the second shift. She gets off at nine. She will not be home until about nine thirty."

"Thank you," said Robert. "Have a nice day." With that they both hung up. Robert then decided to go home and prepare dinner for himself. He would try to call Carmella in the morning.

The next morning Robert went to the police station He walked directly into Bill's office.

"Good morning Bill. How are you this morning?"

"I'm fine," said Bill. "What have you found out about Phil's family?"

"I have only talked with the one sister, whose namem is Natalie Lopez. Her son and daughter both live somewhereout west and they are all Born-Again-Christians. I don't see that they would have anything to do with the murders. "I am going to call the other sister, Carmela later this morning. She works at a restaurant and works till nine in the evening."

"So what do you think we should do next?" asked Bill.

"You are the leader of this case, remember" said Robert. "I am only the assistant."

"As the assistant I am asking you for your opinion," said Bill with a smirk on his face.

"I think we should wait till I talk to Carmela," said Robert. "I have a feeling that our answer is there."

"Well carry on assistant," said Bill getting back at Robert. He knew that Robert was only joking. Robert went into the main office and had a cup of coffee. He wanted to wait until he thought that Carmela was up and around that morning. At about ten he called her.

"Hello," said a woman's voice. "This is Carmela. Who am I talking to?" she asked.

"This is Detective Robert Bensen. I would like to talk to you about your brother Philip."

"Yes my sister told me about the death of our brother and his wife. I was very shock to hear about it."

"I would like to know all that you know about them," said Robert. "We loved our brother, but his wife made it hard for us to see him," said Carmela. "We haven't seen him since his first anniversary." "I understand that you sent your son to ask for financial help," said Robert."

"Yes we were hoping that Phil could lend us some money," you see my husband come down with lung cancer. It is one of the worse kinds. I took him to the cancer hospital in Chicago for treatment. It kept him alive for a few months but then he died. It cost me everything I had. I had gotten a large house mortgage and I could not borrow any more. I needed help and I still do. I am working twelve hours a day to get enough money to keep my house. I am still close to losing it. My son Benny went to ask for a loan. Phil however was not home so he begged Dolores. She would not give him anything."

"I understand that Phil gave your son some money," said Robert." "Yes," said Carmela. "Bennie called Phil on his cell phone. Phil met him at his bank and took out all he had and gave it to Bennie.

That would pay one month of our house mortgage." "Where is your son?" asked Robert.

"I don't know," said Carmela. "I was lucky to find him to send him to see his Uncle Phil. Since his dad died he has been hard to handle. The last time I talked to him he said he was going to look for a job in Ohio. He said he didn't want to be a burden on me. He is aware of the debt that I'm in. The last job he had was as a delivery boy. He since quit that job. What I am saying is that I don't know where he is. He is twenty eight years old. I have no control over him."

"How is his temper," asked Robert. "Is he capable to get in a fit of anger capable to harm anyone?"

"I guess I should tell you, because you will find out soon anyway," said Carmela. "He was in jail for three months on charges of beating up a fellow at a bar and putting him in the hospital. He just got so mad that he would not stop beating the fellow, even when he was down and unconscious. I pray that he is not involved in this in any way."

"Thank you very much for your honesty," said Robert. "You are right; I did look up his record." Robert lied. He had no idea that Ben had been in trouble. He said that to let her be aware that he was a suspect. It would be easier on her in the long run. Robert thought that it was very possible that Ben had murdered his aunt and uncle.

The funeral was to take place in two days. They had a lot of work to do before then. Bill called together the two lawyers, Dolores's lawyer and Philip's lawyer that were listed in the wills. It was interesting that they both have different lawyers. Bill also asked Robert to attend.

"The reason I call you two together," said Bill, "is to discuss the last will and testaments of the two victims. I also want to discuss the special signed document." They all read the document and finally decided to discuss what each believed. Everyone agreed that the special document referred only if the two were to divorce. Since this was not the case they all agree that the document was not valid. Then they looked at the last will of Dolores.

"It says that if she dies first that she leaves everything to Philip," said Ralph Brown Dolores's lawyer. "It does not say anything about if they die together."

"I think that Dolores died first," said Peter Lane, Phil's lawyer, "even if it was just a few minutes before Philip." They did discuss it for a few minutes then they agreedthat Dolores did die first.

"I will have to discuss this with Dolores's family said Ralph. "I understand that she has a cousin named Sylvia."

"If I understand everything that we have discussed, the will Of Philip will be the only one that will be followed," said Peter. "Of course we have to inform the family members to see if they will agree. Then if we all agree this meeting is over," said Robert, "After the Pastor says the prayer at the funeral showing, which  I understand will be one day only, before every one leaves let's get everyone together. All of us and all the members of Dolores and Philips family." They all agreed and left the meeting. Two days later the two, Dolores, and Philip were displayed at the funeral home. All family members of both were present. Bill and Robert were also there. They also had police at the entrance and at the parking lot. About a half hour after the funeral parlor opened Phyllis Carson, the victim's neighbor, showed up. She walked right up to Robert.

"Hi Detective Bensen," said Phyllis. "When I got here I noticed a black foreign car in the parking lot. I recognized it as the car that was at Dolores's house the day they got shot. I recognized it because seeing it I remembered that it had a damaged back fender. I had forgotten that when I talked with you the other day"

"Thank you so much Phyllis," said Robert. "Please call me Robert. I am retired now." After she said a prayer at the coffins she went and sat down near a woman that Robert suspected was Sylvia. Robert then called the police officer that was in the parking lot.

"Officer Brian," ordered Robert, "look for a black foreign car with a damaged left back fender. If anyone goes to it arrest him and  call me." Robert noticed that there were four women, one older man and two young boys. One of the women and the older man sat together. Next to them was another woman. Robert figured that these were Phil's two sisters and the husband of the older sister. The neighbor Phyllis was sitting by herself. Robert didn't know who the two younger men where. They were sitting alone by themselves. When he went to talk to the one that was closer he notice that the one who was near the door got up and left. He prooceeded to go to the one young man that was left. On the way he got a phone call from Officer Brian.

"There was a young man who started to open the door to the black car," said Brian. "When I approached him he started to run. I caught him and am taking him to the police station."

"That is great," said Robert. "Just hold him. I will come as soon as I can get away." When Robert got to the young man he sat next to him.

"Hi,' said Robert, "I'm detective Robert Bensen. I'm trying to learn all that I can about Philip and Dolores Bladen. Do you mind telling me who you are and how you know them?"

"Hi, my name is Nick MacForen. I was a good friend of Phil. I've known him since high school."

"I think we should talk in the office across the hall," said Robert. "Do you mind coming with me. I think you can tell me a lot about them." On the way Robert stopped to inform Bill of what he was doing.

"Do you want to come with us?"

"No you go ahead," said Bill. "I think one of us should stay here." Robert then took Nick to the office.

"Please sit here by the table," said Robert. "Please tell me what you know of your and their relationship."

"As I said I knew Phil from high school," started Nick. "We went to ball games together; we even went on double dates together. However, after he got married I didn't see him very often. His wife looked down on me as being below their level. She was a very arrogant woman. I don't think Phil should have married her. He was so different from her. He was so kind and big hearted. However he was crazy in love with her."

"When was the last time you saw him?" asked Robert.

"I hadn't seen him in over a year when suddenly a few days ago he showed up at my door step. I asked him in and he told me that he was going to divorce, Dolores. I asked why and he told me that she accused him of marrying her for her money. He said that he was going to divorce her to prove that he didn't give a darn for her money. He told me that he had signed an agreement that if they got divorced he would get nothing. I am a Christian and I don't believe in divorce. As much as I didn't like her I tried to talk him to go back and make up with her."

"How long," asked Robert, did he stay with you?"

"He was here for about two days. I finally talked him in going back and apologize and get back together. I wish I had not done that. If I hadn't talked him into going back he probably would still be alive."

"Thank you so much," said Robert. "Please go back and spend the last few hours with Phil." Nick left and went back to sit in the front row. Robert then went to talk with Bill.

"Bill," said Robert. "I got a call from Officer Brian. He has captured the owner of the black car and has taken him to the police station. Do you want to go and interrogate him?"

"No you go ahead," said Bill. "I think I better stay here. They were your assignment. I think the lawyers and I will talk to the family of each and tell them of our finding."

"All right," said Robert. "I'll keep you informed" Robert then left for the police station. At the police station he asked that Ben be brought into the interrogation room.

Please sit at the end of the table," said Robert to Ben as soon as he was brought into the room. This young lady with us is Amanda. She will take notes of everything that happens in here. She also has a hand held recorder.

"Why am I here?" said Ben trying to look innocent.

"You are being charged with the murder of Philip and Dolores Bladen," said Robert.

"I didn't do it," said Ben. "What makes you think that I did it? What evidence do you have?"

"First of all your car was identified as the car that was there at the time of the shooting. The damaged back fender gave you away. A neighbor who heard the shootings saw your car there. Secondly your finger prints are all over the furniture of their house, that shouldn't be there especially in their bed room.It was evident that you were looking for their last will and testament and their special inheritance agreement." Ben looked like hewas ready to cry. "Look," said Robert. "If you confess and tell us what happened then you might get a better deal."

"I didn't mean to kill them," said Ben now in tears. "Tell us exactly what happened," said Robert.

"I went there to beg her to help my mother," started Ben. "I told her that my mother could lose her house. She got very nasty and asked me to leave. I begged her to listen and that I would make any deal she wanted. She grabbed me and tied to kick me out of her house. I resisted. She then headed for her bedroom. I follow just behind her begging all the way. I had no idea of what she had on her mind. When she got there she opened a drawer and pulled out a gun. She said that she would claim that I had broken in and she had to protect herself.

When she pointed the gun at me I grabbed it and tried to take it away from her. The gun went off. It hit her in the chest."

"There is evidence that the bullet entered at an angle and that her dress had gun powder burns on it. That may help you a little; however that doesn't explain why you killed Philip."

"I didn't want to kill him," said Ben. "He was my blood uncle. He came in after I spent some time looking for the inheritance documents. He attacked me when he walked in and saw what I was doing. I don't understand why since she was such a terrible person, but he must have loved her very much. Since I knew where I had left the gun, I got it and used it to protect myself."

"I don't know if any of this will hold up in court as a defense," said Robert. "But we will provide this information to the prosecutor. We will provide a defense lawyer if you can't afford one. Since you have confessed I think it will be just a session with the judge." Robert then turned the procedure to the prosecuting attorney. Even though Robert sat in on the session he was not involved in the case after that. It was after four that he was able to leave.

Meanwhile at the funeral parlor, the lawyers had contacted all the family members who they felt would expect some inheritance from the death of Philip and Dolores. They were told to meet across the hall from the display area after the final prayer. It happened at about four thirty that a minister came in and gave the final prayer. After he was done, and every one left the area, all the family members went into the room across the hall. There were seven people all together. After they all walked in, Peter Lane, who was Philip's lawyer, address them.

"Please everyone have a seat anywhere around the table.

"I will be the spokesman at this meeting," said Peter. After they all sat down he continued. "My name is Peter Lane. I am Philip's lawyer.

"Starting at my left please state your name and how you are related to the Phil and Dolores."

"My name is Sylvia Howe," said the first person on Peter's left. I am the first cousin of Dolores."

"My name is Carmela Sherman," said the next person. "I am Phil's sister."

"My name is Natalie Lopez," said the next person. "I am also Phil's sister."

"My name is Tony Lopez. I am Natalie's husband."

"My name is Ralph Brown," said the next person. "I am Dolores's attorney."

"I am William Bradman," said the last person. "I am a police officer. I'm here to record all the details of the meeting."

"Thank you all," said Peter, "Well then let's continue this meeting. We are mostly here to inform you of the results we came up with at a preliminary meeting after studying all the documents. We need the approval of the results we came up with from all of you. We are also here to hear your comments.

First we reviewed the special document with an agreement which they both sign. They document was about the distribution of their possessions if they go divorced. Since they were not divorced it is no longer valid. Does anyone have any comments?" No one spoke. "Therefore let's go on to the next document. It is the last will and testament of Dolores. If she died before Philip, it states that all her possessions will go to Philip. Since she died before Philip even though it was only around an hour, we feelthat she did die before Phil. Do you Sylvia have any objection to this concussion?"

"I want you to understand something," said Ralph. "My client has no inclination to claim any inheritance no matter what the outcome of this meeting will be. She thinks that all of Phil and Dolores's possessions should go to Phil's sisters."

"That is very kind of you," said Carmela. "We are very grateful. God Bless you."

"We would also like to be excused from this meeting. I don't see that we could add anything," said Ralph.

"I also want to say that it looks like everything is going the way I wanted it to go. God has blessed me with more then I deserve. So God bless you all." With that said they both got up and left.

Well the last item is Philip's will," said Peter. "It is pretty clear. It leaves everything to his two sisters. I will see that all is distributed equally to both of you. Therefore, I recommend that after the burial tomorrow you go to the funeral parlor and eat lunch there. After the lunch you come to my office. There we will sign all the necessary paper. After that I will take you to the bank and transfer all the money to both of you."

"I have two questions said Carmela. "First who is paying for the funeral and who is paying you?"

"The funeral and burial is paid for by the insurance they had for this purpose. As for me they had set aside a bank account for this purpose. Now I have a question. Do you have a stock brooker that can handle the stocks that you two will inherent?"

"I have stock broker that handles my investment," small as they are," said Natalie.

"By the way," asked Carmela, "how much money are we talking about?"

"It will amount to a little over three million dollars," said Peter. The girls looked like they were going to faint.

"Here is what I recommend," said Bill. "After you get all the paper completed, go home and get you stockbroker to set everything up for both of you. After all you accounts are fixed one of you should come back here to sell all the furniture and finally the house. I suggest that person be you Natalie, since you have no one that you would be leaving behind."

"I think that is a great idea," said Peter. "And while you're here if you need anything I will be at your service." The two sisters looked at each other and they both said that they agreed with the plan. That done they all left. Bill felt like his job was complete. He decided that he would not be needed anymore. He left with a feeling of success.

Robert finished all that was required and went into Captain Wilson's office.

"Well Captain," said Robert. "I think my job is complete. He then explained to the Captain all that had happened."

"I know," said the Captain. "The prosecuting attorney has kept me updated."

"Well then I believe that I am no longer need," said Robert. "You did a great, job as I expected," said the Captain. "I promise not to call except in an extreme emergency."

"That is what you said the last time," said Robert with laughter in his voice.

"Go home and have a great retired life," said the Captain. Robert left for home. On the way home he had a happy feeling. Life was going to be peaceful and serene. Robert had no idea of what the future would bring.

# THE UNEXPECTED EMERGENCY

ROBERT FELT AT EASE since his assignment was over. He felt free from having to solving another case. Not only that but he felt inspired to work on his novel The experience he got from solving the last cases gave him some great ideas for his novel. It was almost like his life history, however he did change some of the details to make it more interesting and of course he did not use any names of people in his cases. He finished chapter four and was sitting quietly trying to come up with the title for chapter five when he heard a knocking on the front door. He got up and walked to the door.

"I wonder who in the world that could be?" he said aloud to himself. "I hope it isn't someone who needs help from a private detective." He was remembering the day that Annie came to his door for help. He opened the door and was socked at who he saw. He was speechless.

"Hi Dad," said Liana. "I thought I would come home and spend a little time with you."

"I have never had a better gift in all my life except the time you were born."

"I decided to take a two week spring break," said Liana. "I missed you and I missed being home. I also have a surprise for you."

"What kind of a surprise are you talking about?" asked Robert.

"You have to wait," said Liana. "It will be delivered to your door sometime today."

"I can hardly wait," said Robert. "Can I try to guess?" "You will never guess what it is," said Liana.

"Is it something," asked Robert, "that comes in a box or does it come in an envelope?"

"You will never guess," said Liana with a great smile on her face. "It will come in a very beautiful package. You will love the package."

"Well tell me about your school and your summer job," said Robert.

"Well my school is fantastic. I can't believe all the progress that has been made. I am learning so much. My grades are greaat. If it keeps up I may keep going to get a doctorate degree.

"That would be so great," said Robert. "I am so proud of you." "As far as my job at the hospital," continued Liana, "it is also very educational. They did give me a hard time when I asked to take a spring break. I thought they wanted to fire me. I however talked them into giving me the time off. The other day when we had a periodic review they said that I was very talented and they were very happy to have me. So I figured that if I was doing such a good job at such a low salary that they would not fire me. So here I am."

"That sounds great," said Robert. For the next few hours they spent the time talking. Robert told her about his experience with the murder of the husband and wife. It was after eleven when Robert started to think about lunch. So he asked Liana, "What would you like for lunch?"

"Dad, let's wait a little while. I'm not too hungry right now. I'm too tired from my trip." It was only a few minutes later that there was a knock at the door.

"I wonder who that is," said Robert as he walked to the door.

"I think it is your surprise gift," said Liana. Robert opened the door. Again he was in a state of shock.

"Hi Dad," said Amy. "May I come in?" Robert couldn't speak so he just grabbed her and hugged her affectionately.

"Hi Sis," said Liana." She then also hugged Amy. "Come on in, Dad is in a state of shock. He will get over it soon."

"You girls are going to give me a heart attack," said Robert. "You mean that you didn't like my gift," said Liana joking at her father's comment.

"I have never had a more beautiful gift in all my life," said Robert with tears in his eyes.

"All of a sudden I am very hungry," said Liana. Robert did not have anything special. He had no idea that he would have company. He took out a loaf of bread and some turkey balcony. He also found that he had some ham.

"I'm sorry girls but I only have lunch meat. If I kneew you were coming I would have cooked something special"

"This is fine Dad," said Liana. "Amy and I will cook something special for you while we are here. Since I live alone I have tried many new recipes that I think you will love."

"What have you heard from Lorrie?" asked Amy. "Is she still in Indiana?"

"No, said Robert. "She has moved here in Ohio. But she is very busy and I have only seen her twice and both times in a store."

"I thought that yoou two had something special going on," said Liana. "I'm surprised that you two haven't gotten together."

"She moved up here and I suspect that she got most of her memory back and went back to being the girl she was. So what do you girls want to do first while you are home?"

"You know Dad," said Amy. "I love the word home. That is exactly how I feel when I am here."

"I think we should spend a day with Grandma and Grandfather," said Liana. "I miss them and I'm sure they would like to see us too."

"I think that is a great idea," said Amy. "I would like them to see me as a Granddaughter."

"That is a great idea," said Robert. "However, I think we should just relax and enjoy each other today."

The next day they got up late, ate breakfast and relaxed until noon. After lunch they went to Robert's parent's house. Robert knocked on the door. Robert's mother opened the door. When she saw Robert she yelled 'hi' and grabbed Robert and hugged him.

"This is the most wonderful surprise I ever got," she said with a very happy expression on her face. "Come on in."

"Hi Mom," said Robert. "I'm sure you remember Amy, my unofficial adopted daughter. And of course you know your granddaughter. They are home on spring break." Robert's mother hugged both girls.

"Come in and have a seat at the kitchen table," said Roberts mom. "I will get you some coffee. It is a strange thing that you came today. I made some Giamelotti that you love so much."

"Wow," said Robert. "Will miracles never end?"

"I never hear of that cookie," said Amy. "It sounds like it is an Italian recipe."

"It is," said Robert's mom. "It was a recipe given me by my grandma. She was a Sicilian." They each took a cookie and a cup of coffee.

"That is the most delicious cookie I ever tasted," said Amy. "You have to give me the recipe."

"I have another miracle today," said Robert's mom. "I am making another Sicilian specialty that you love. It is almost like I knew you were coming. I have enough sauce for five people."

"I'm sorry Mom," said Robert. "We did not intend to stay for dinner. We planned on only staying for a couple of hours."

"First of all," said Roberts's mother, "You have to stay to see your father. He will be home soon. He would be devastated if he missed seeing you all."

"I was wondering where he was," said Robert.

"He went out to buy something for this evening. Knowing him he will buy enough for all of us. Anyway the second reason you will not leave is that I will not let you leave. However, I don't think that would be a big job. You see what I am cooking for tonight is Cavatelli with pork neck bones."

"After all that," said Liana, "how can we possibly leave?" About fifteen minutes later Robert's father came home. He was more surprised than his wife Liana had been. One at a time he hugged them all.

"It is so good to see you all," said Joseph. Joseph then spent the time till dinner asking the girls about their experience at school and at their jobs. Soon it was dinner time. Robert's mom set a dish of Cavatelli in front of each and then set a large plate of meat balls and a large plate of pork neck bones in the center of the table. They all ate the Cavatelli and each took a meat ball with the Cavatelli. After finishing the Cavatelli, Robert's father grabbed two pork neck bones.e Roberts's mother didn't take any but she did take more meat balls. Liana and Amy took one pork neck bones to see how they would like them. They loved them and soon each took another one. They all finally finished dinner.

"When," asked Roberts mother, "do you want dessert?" "Tomorrow," said Robert. "I don't think I will have room until then."

"We will wait until later," said Robert's mother. She then left the room for a few minutes. It was almosteight thirty when they all agreed to eat dessert. Robert's mom brought out a chocolate cake. They all had a small peace with a cup of coffee. When they had finished the dessert Robert got up.

"I think me and girls have to go home." They hugged and said goodbye. Robert's mom led them to the door.

"By the way," she said before they left, "when I left the room I called your sister Teresa. She has invited you to her house for dinner. Please go. You don't want to hurt her feelings." Robert shook his forefinger at her as they left.

The next morning they slept until nine and then got up and had breakfast.

"Do you girls want to go to my sister's house for dinner?" asked Robert.

"I think we had better go," said Liana. "Just think how disappointed she would be. Besides she would be very hurt. Why did you have anything else in mind?"

"I agree with you," said Robert. "We have to go. I was planning on taking you girls to Cedar Point Park for the day."

"There are two reasons why we can't go to Cedar Point," said Amy. "First I agree we have to go to Aunt Teresa. Secondly I was up earlier then you guys so I went into the TV room and watched the news. The weather man said that it was going to rain this afternoon in western Ohio. That is where Cedar Point is isn't it?"

"That settles it then," said Robert. "We will leave for my sister Teresa's house after lunch." The next day as Robert had decided they left for Teresa's house.

"Teresa had expected them and she opened the door as they went up the front porch.

"Hi you guys," said Teresa. "It's so nice to see you guys. I haven't seen you since the fourth on July last year. Come on in. Make yourselves at home." They all walked in and were each individually hugged. They sat in the living room and relaxed.

"Now tell me," said Teresa, "what have you girls been up to?" Liana started first. She told her about the college courses she was taking and all about the experience she got at the hospital.

"How about you," said Liana, "What have you been doing?"

"I have been working at Ken Stewarts for twelve years," said Teresa. "I am a waitress. I usually work until nine, but I took a day off." "I think your boss is not very happy," said Robert. "Fridays and Saturdays are the busiest days in most restaurants."

"Yes," said Teresa. "My boss wasn't too happy. But I have been one of the most reliable in the restaurant. How about you Amy? What have you been doing?"

"My story is almost identical to Liana's story." said Amy. "The only difference is that she works in a hospital in Columbus, and goes to school at Ohio State, and I work at University Hospital and go to school at Cleveland State."

"What do you girls plan on doing the rest of time that you are in this area?" asked Teresa.

"I was going to take them to Cedar Point tomorrow," said Robert." "Can I make a suggestion?" asked Teresa. "Sure," said Robert. "What do you suggest?"

"I suggest that you wait until Monday to go to Cedar Point.

Saturdays and Sundays will be the most crowded days of the week. That is when most people have time off from work."

"I think you are right," said Robert. "We will wait until Monday." The rest of the afternoon was passed with small talk and a few jokes by Robert. At about five thirty Teresa came in with the most delicious pizza that they ever tasted. The evening ended with strawberry cake and coffee. They went home with joy in their hearts.

The next day was Saturday. They all slept in late. The girls after a small breakfast decided to spend the day just wandering at the mall.

"Do you girls need some cash?" asked Robert. "I can give you my credit card."

"I have more money then I deserve," said Amy. "Besides I have a credit card of my own."

"How about you Liana?" asked Robert. "What are your thoughts?" "I don't need anything," said Liana. "I am just going to look around. I'm just going with Amy to keep her company."

"Here take my credit card just in case you find something you want," saidRobert.

"If she needs something," said Amy. I will buy it for my sister." Liana took the credit card anyway. They had lunch at the mall and come home at super time. The next day was Sunday. They went to church and came home to a juicy steak lunch. That afternoon, Amy and Liana played cards to pass the time.

Monday morning they all got up early. They ate a quick breakfast and soon headed for Cedar Point. It took a little over an hour before they found themselves entering the parking lot.

"Wow," said Liana, "The parking lot is very full for a Monday." "Imagine how full it would have been Saturday, when a lot more people were home from work." said Robert. Inside they found it more crowded then they wanted.

"Look at the long lines at each of the rides," said Amy. "I think we should go and visit all the booths until later."

"That is an excellent suggestion," said Liana. "I don't want to spend all day in lines."

"Let's walk around and visit the action booths," said Robert. "I see the rifle booth. Let's see if either of you can win a doll." After Robert paid the fee, Liana tried first. She had never shot a rifle before. It showed. She missed the target by a mile.

"Let's see what you can do Daddy," said Liana.

"No I don't think that would be fair or honest," said Robert. "I was a police officer. I spent hours firing a rifle. How about you Amy would you like to try?"

"I went a couple of time to a rifle range with my father," admitted Amy. "I was only about eight. However, I would like to give it a try." Robert paid the fee and Amy took the rifle and aiming carefully took a shot. It came so close it almost skimmed the edge of the target.

"That was very good," said Robert. "I think you need a second try." After Robert paid the fee Amy took a second shot. This time she hit the target right in the middle. She earned a doll. She picked a fuzzy little bear. After that, they circled around all the booths. After they had lunch, theytried several other games with no success. It was about four when they noticed that the lines at the rides got much smaller. Soon they were trying all the rides. They liked the roller coaster best because Robert rode with them. When it was after seven they decided that they had enough. On the way home they stopped at Chilies restaurant for dinner. They liked the Baby Back Pork Rib dinner at chilies. After diner they went home. They were too tired to do anything but watch TV. Robert fell asleep in the middle of the movie.

The next day was Tuesday. It was a very beautiful day. Robert suggested that they have a picnic on such a beautiful day. Besides he was tired of traveling. They all agreed. After breakfast they packed a basket full of two different sandwiches and left for Sand Run Park. They found a nice clearing and laid a blanket on the grass and set up for lunch. After lunch Liana and Amy walked to the open field by a small river. Liana had brought a soft ball and two baseball gloves. Liana and Amy played throwing the ball to each other. Liana would sometimes throw the ball high in the air. Amy had no problem catching it. Sometimes Amy would do the same thing to Liana. Sometimes they would throw the ball as hard as they could like a pitcher would. They enjoyed the day very much. They asked Robert to join them but he decided to read a magazine instead. The  day was very enjoyable to all three of them.

On Wednesday after breakfast Liana approached her dad. "Dad," she started, "this is Wednesday and I would like it to be girl's day. You know that we have been in contact with two of the girls that I went to high school with. One is a receptionist for Doctor Bower and the other is the assistant to Doctor Barnum. They are all closed on Wednesday. So I would like to spend the day with them."

"That would be fine with me," said Robert. "What do you think about that Amy?"

"I'm fine with that," said Amy. "You go and have fun with your friends."

"No way," said Liana. "You are coming with me. I would like them to meet my new sister."

"I wouldn't want to be a drag on you," said Amy. "You go with your friends."

Well," said Liana. "If you don't want to go I will not go either. I will not leave you."

"Since you put it that way," said Amy. "When do you want to go?" "We will go about three this afternoon," said Liana. They left  at exactly three. Robert didn't know what the girls were going to do. He didn't want to know. He just wanted them to come home safely. Robert went to bed at eleven thirty. The girls had not come home. The next morning at breakfast he asked the girls about how they spent yesterday.

"We spent the afternoon just shooting the bull," said Liana.

"It was so interesting to hear about the jobs the girls were doing," said Amy. "It gives me some thought about what I want to do with my life."

"After that," continued Liana, "we went to dinner at a Cleveland night club that had a band and a bar. We got home a little after twelve." After breakfast Liana made a request.

"You know Dad," she said, "We were in such a hurry when we were at the Cleveland Zoo that we missed some of the last part of the zoo. I would like to go back and spend more time and see the part of the zoo we missed."

"Whatever you guys want to do is alright with me," said Robert. "I think it is a good idea," said Amy. "We were in a huurry to go to grandma's house."

"Well this time we will not tell Grandma that we are going," said Robert. "We can go tomorrow morning and spend all day there." Early Friday morning they had a quick and simple breakfast and soon were at the Cleveland Zoo. As they entered they went by the gorilla cage.

"Now Dad," said Liana wanting to kid her dad. "Please don't go into the gorilla cage like you did the last time we were here."

"Very funny," said Robert. It was not however funny to Robert. It reminded him too much of Lorrie. They walked through all the places they had spent time the last time they were there and spent more time at the areas they had not visited. They enjoyed watching the elephants and the kangaroos. At noon they had a sandwich and then went back visiting all the animals. Amy enjoyed watching the giraffes. She couldn't believe how long their necks were. She had only seen pictures before. The real live giraffes were much more exciting. The pictures did not portray how big the giraffes really were. Seeing one in real life is the only way that can one really appreciate the size of the giraffe. It was the size that excited Amy. They spent all day seeing everything that was there to see. It was very late when they decided to go home. On the way home they stopped at the Red Lobster restaurant for dinner. It was almost nine thirty. But they were hungry. Robert ordered shrimp with angel hair pasta. It sounded good to Amy she had the same thing. Liana had salmon. After eating they went home. They were very tired but extremely happy.

Saturday they stayed home and enjoyed each other's company. The girls decided to play cards. They had a game called Uno. The girls were getting sad because they realized that in a day they will not see each other. They had feeling for each other like real sisters. The card games kept their minds off the coming separation. Robert could feel their sadness as well as his own. Saturday went by too soon. Soon it was Sunday morning and they all went to church. They all had faith that God will see them through the separation. After they came home Robert made a steak for each on the grill. After lunch Lianna stayed for a while but soon she had to leave. She had the farthest to travel.

"Dad," said Liana, as she went to the doorway to leave. "Thank you so much for having me and giving me the best time of my life. You are the best father a girl could have. I will try to get home for the holidays" Robert hugged her with tears in his eyes. When she walked to her car Amy went with her. Robert stayed inside. He wanted the girls to have the time together. A few minutes later Amy came back inside.

"I hope you will stay until after super," said Robert. "Both of you leaving at the same time will be too hard to take."

"I will stay until after dinner. We both need each other for a while." They spent the afternoon reliving the time they sent together the last two weeks. For dinner Robert made Tilapia fish. Amy loved it. Soon it was time for Amy to leave. They hugged and Robert spoke his last words.

"Good bye Amy, please always remember that I love you like a real daughter."

"Goodbye Dad," said Amy as she left for her car. "Remember that I love you like my real father." A few minutes later she was gone. Robert went inside and never felt as sad before as he did at that time.

Monday Robert got up late, ate breakfast and tried to work on his computer. Somehow, he felt like he didn't want to think. He had a sort of what they call author mental block. He couldn't think of what to write next in his novel. Finally he got up and turned on the TV. He had to get over his problem. He was sure that he didn't want to think because it brought up the girls who he missed terribly. That night he went to bed early. On Tuesday morning he felt better. He ate breakfast and went to his computer. He was stuck on where his mystery was going to take place. Soon it was lunch time. He had a small sandwich and went back to his computer. It was about two in the afternoon that he got a call from Captain Wilson.

"Hi Robert," said the Captain. "How are you? Don't worry this is not an assignment. I am just going over the records over the last few months and I have some question about the assignments you were on. I would ask Bill but he is out of town. Do you think that you could take a few minutes and help me go over the records?"

"I'd love to," said Robert. "I'm having a problem getting over my daughters who were here for their spring break. They just left Sunday. I could use the distraction. How soon do you want me to come over?" "How about right now," said the Captain. "I have everything out on my desk. I will only take a few minutes."

"I'll be right there," said Robert. He got his car keys and left immediately. At the Captain's office they reviewed all the records.

Robert found the place that troubled the Captain. He corrected the record and spent somme time talking about what was going on since Robert left the police job. It was about four thirty when Robert got home. He was very excited because the thought of the girls and where they spent the last two week along with the records he reviewed gave him an Idea on how to create the mystery and where it could take place. He felt very excited about what was on his mind for the next part of his novel. He couldn't wait to get in on the computer. He quickly went on the computer and work diligently to set up the mystery. Once he had the mystery set up, he worked on how to get his imaginary detective to solve the mystery. He was so involved in what he was doing that he lost all track of time.

When he finished the solving of the mystery he looked at his watch.

"Holy smoke," he said out loud. "It is almost eight o'clock." He then went to the refrigerator to see what he could cook for dinner. He found that everything he had was in the freezer. He decided he wanted fish. He had not had fish since the first week that the girls were home. Then he had second thoughts about cooking his fish. First he would have to thaw it out. Then he would have to cook it. He decided that it was too late to do all that work. He finally decided to go out to eat. He decided to go to Red Lobster for the fish dinner he loved. He got into his car and five minutes later he was at Red Lobster. He walked into the door and walked up to the counter. The young lady at the counter who was looking at a chart looked up at Robert.

"Good evening," she said, "how many will there be?"

"Just me," said Robert. Then looking at the dinner tables he saw Lorrie at one of the tables by the window. "Never mind, I see a friend of mine siting by the window. I will go and sit with her." Robert then walked up to the table where Lorrie was sitting.

"Good evening, Lorrie," he said and started to sit across from her. "Please go away," she said. "Please don't sitdown. I don't want to be with you."

"I will gladly go away but not until you tell me what I did wrong. Why are you angry with me?"

"I don't want to talk about it," said Lorrie, "so go away."

"I will not go away until you tell me what I did that has made you so unfriendly."

"Why," asked Lorrie, "do you insist on hurting me?" "How am I hurting you?" asked Robert. "You are hurting me just being here." "Just tell me what I did and I will go away," said Robert.

"You didn't do anything wrong," said Lorrie. "The problem is me. I understand that you have your life and I have mine."

"Did you get your memory back?" asked Roberts, "and that has made you a different person."

"I don't really know if I got my memory back," said Lorrie. "I went through all the folders I had in my desk and filing cabinet. I don't know if I remembered or relived it by reading about my history."

"Well if I didn't do anything wrong," said Robert. "If you don't have any feelings for me, why can't we just be friends?"

"We could never be friends," said Lorrie, with small tears showing in her eyes. Just then the waitress walked.

"Are you ready to order?" said the waitress. "I will have you salmon dinner," said Lorrie.

"I will have your shrimp with angel hair pasta," said Robert. "What do you want to drink?" asked the waitress.

"I will just have a glass of water," said Robert.

"I will have a cup of coffee," said Lorrie. After the waitress walked away Robert turned back to Lorrie.

"Where were we?" asked Robert. "Oh yes, I was asking why can't we be friends?"

"I can't be friends with someone who broke my heart," said Lorrie now looking down on the table trying to hide the sadness in her face from Robert. Before Robert could answer, the waitress brought them their food. After the waitress left Robert answered Lorrie.

"I'm completely lost now," said Robert. "I don't know anything more now than I did when I first got here. How did I break your heart? I tried to call you several times. But I always got the same answer. They said that the phone was no longer active. I was hoping that you would reinstate the phone so that I could talk to you."

"Why didn't you call me on my cell phone?" asked Lorrie.

"You just got your cell phone the day before I took you home to Indiana. Remember also that the phone battery was dead."

"You could have found a way," said Lorrie. "It was only a few months and you forgot me and started running around with other women."

"What makes you think I was running around with other women?" asked Robert.

"I always believed that you were a sweet honest person. But I was wrong. You are lying to me right now."

"What am I lying about?" asked Robert. "I have not been running around with other girls. I have nor even seen one since I brought you to Indiana."

"See that," said Lorrie beginning to get angry. "You are lying right now. I saw you with another girl."

"I think you were dreaming," said Robert. "Let's start from the begging. Tell me every step you took since I left you in Indiana."

"All right," said Lorrie. "I think this is the only way that I am going to get rid of you. You're not going to give up."

"No," said Robert. "I will not give up until I find out what this is all about."

"When you left me in Indiana," started Lorrie, "I was sad to see you go. I was going to miss you."

"I know said Robert. "I looked out the front window as I was backing out and saw you standing there looking very sad."

"After you left, I and Melanie got together and she brought me up to date as to what happened in the past. I also went through all my document and possessionsand gota good feeling as to who I was. Then with the help of a friend who was a real estate agent we set a price on all the furniture I didn't want and had a red flag day. We sold all the furniture I didn't want except the worn out couch. I then hired a fellow with a truck and together we brought the furniture and possessions I wanted to keep to my bungalow. Before I did this I had an interview by phone and got a job and also rented a bungalow. That is where I brought all my furniture. I then went back with the truck driver to sell my house. After I sold my house I left Indiana for good. I then drove my car to my home in Ohio. On the way I decided to stop and see you. I pulled up on you turn around and knocked on the door. No one answered, so I walked to your back yard. I thought that being such a nice day that you might be in the back yard where I knew you had a grill. It was dinner time so I thought you might be cooking dinner on your grill. That's when I saw a woman hugging and kissing you. You looked like you were enjoying it. So in just a few months you had found a new sweetheart. I was heartbroken and barely got home." Robert looked at Lorrie and started to laugh heartily. "Why are you laughing," said Lorrie. "Are you making fun of me? Because I caught you into the act you think it is funny?"

"So that is what all this is all about?" asked Robert.

"Do you have feelings for her?" asked Lorrie feeling very jealous. "I have very strong feelings for her," said Robert. "She said that she loved me. However there is a problem with all of this. She is more than ten years younger than me."

"That didn't seem to make a difference to you," said Lorrie. "There is another problem," said Robert. "She loves me because her husband, who is the love of her life, was arrested for the murder of her old boyfriend. She loves me because my investigation found the real killer and she was thanking me for giving her husband back."

"I feel like an idiot," said Lorrie. "Howeverthat doesn't tell me how you feel about me. If you cared about me you would have told me. You never gave an indication that you cared for me."

"How could I tell you anything," said Robert, "We didn't know if you were single or married with a dozen children."

"Are you saying thhat you care for me?" asked Lorrie holding her breath.

"You are an idiot," said Robert. "I think it was pretty obvious from the way I have been fighting for you. I fell in love with you the minute you woke up at the hospital when I first met you. I fell for you when you woke up and said 'Hi' in that beautiful affectionate voice. Can't you tell that I am crazy about you?"

"I fell in love with you when I first woke up," said Lorrie. "I looked up and thought that I had died and was in heaven with an angel looking down at me." Robert joyfully smiled.

"I guess what we are saying is that we are both madly in love with each other," said Robert.

"That is how I see it," said Lorrie. Robert got up and grabbed Lorrie's hand and pulled her up. As soon as she got up he kissed her. It was such a fantastic moment that they didn't hear the clapping that the people around then did when they saw them kissing. It was too late to make plans for that night so after much hugging and kissing they made plans for the next day and each went to their own home. On the way home Robert was happier than he had ever been. He had no idea what the future had in store for them.

# CHAPTER SIX

# AN UNEXPECTED TURN OF EVENTS

ROBERT GOT UP EARLY the next day. He was thrilled at what had happened the night before. He sat at his computer, but he couldn't write. He was thinking that he wantedto spend time with Lorrie. He thought that he could take her to some of the places that he took his girls. The problem was that he didn't know what Lorrie's work schedule was. Could she take time off to visit some of the places he took the girls? He will have to discuss this with her later. At this time he only wanted to see her. He called her when he felt she would be at lunch.

"Hi Lorrie," he said after she answered the phone. "How are you?" I'm fine," she said. "I'm eating my lunch. You called at the right time. I probably would not have answered if I was at work."

"Well I won't keep you long," said Robert. "I just wanted to ask you if you would like to go out this evening."

"I would love that," said Lorrie.

"You get off at four-thirty," said Robert. "Can I pick you up at your job at that time?"

"I'd rather you pick me up at home," said Lorrie. "I need to clean up. I want to look beautiful to you. I think I will want to take a shower before I go out. Come and pick me up at six."

"I just wanted to spend more time with you," said Robert. "Give me your address." Lorrie gave him her address and directions as how to get there. Since Robert had lived in the area most of his life he know exactly where she lived. The hours went by so slowly that day that is seemed like a week to Robert. However the time soon came up. Robert presented himself at her door at exactly six.

"Wow," said Lorrie. "You are exactly on time. Where do you want to go for dinner?"

"I think I would like to go to Olive Garden," said Robert. "They have Chicken Marsala that I love."

"Sounds good to me," said Lorrie. They drove to Olive Garden and were soon settled by a window as Lorrie asked.

"Well here we are together at last," said Robert. "Today went by so slowly that I thought that evening would never come."

"I know," said Lorrie. "I should have let you pick me up at work." "No," said Robert, "this is fine. You would have felt uneasy.

Although you would be beautiful if you just came out of a mud pit." "You are funny," said Lorrie. "Tell me, what have you been doing since you left me in Indiana?" Before he could answer the waitress came for their order. Lorrie looked at the menu and ordered the Chicken Marsala. Robert smiled at her and ordered the same thing. Lorrie also asked for coffee and Robert said he only wanted water.

"So my telling you about the Chicken Marsala," asked Robert, "got you interested did it?"

"Yes it sounded so delicious," said Lorrie, "anyway what have you been up to?"

"Well as I told you yesterday, I freed that young lady's husband. In another case, I found the person who killed a wife and husband to get their inheritance." Robert then told her the whole story. In the meantime the waitress brought them their food.

"This is very delicious," said Lorrie as she ate the food. "I will have to listen to you often."

Tell me about your new job," said Robert. "You have not told me anything about it."

"My new job is in the University Hospital" said Lorrie. I work in the lab. I am the head nurse. I perform tests on patient sent down by the doctors that have offices in the building. There are five different electrical devices I run."

I understand that you were a surgeon's assistant back in Indiana. What does that mean?"

"I have a master's degree in nursing. That puts me above

a regular nurse's level but below the doctor's level. I am referred to as a Nurse practitioner."

"Sound like a very interesting and exciting job," said Robert.

"I handle a lot different types of medical problems in the lab," said Lorrie.

"I see that we are almost done with our dinner," said Robert. "What do you think about going to the movie theater that is just a little distance from here? There is a very exciting detective movie being run there."

If you don't mind," said Lorrie, "I would rather go to your house and see a movie on your TV.

"If that is what you want then let's do it," said Robert. When they got home Robert selected a movie from his DVD collection that Lorrie liked and he turned it on. They never saw the movie. They were in each other's arms and spent the rest of the evening savoring each other's lips. At about eleven Lorrie pulled herself away.

"Oh Robert," she said. "I have to go to work tomorrow. I have to get up around six. I will get less than six hours sleep. Please take me home." Robert and Lorrie got into Robert's car and started to go to Lorrie home. On the way Robert decided to make future plans.

"Lorrie, can I pick you up at six tomorrow?"

Oh Robert," said Lorrie. "I have so much work to do at home. I have several bills to pay. Tomorrow is Thursday, so why don't you pick me up at six on Friday?"

"That sounds great," said Robert. "However it will seem like a week to me."

"I know," said Lorrie. "To me too, But I'm still settling in. I was so busy getting familiar with the lab that I stayed over time to study the equipment."

"I understand," said Robert. "I will miss you." Lorrie smiled as they got to her house. She bent over and gave Robert a goodnight kiss and got out of the car. Robert went home feeling very happy. The next morning Robert got up early. He had his breakfast and left for Marconi's Jewelry Store. At the store he reviewed all the engagement rings that they had. He finally chose a three and a half carat diamond that he loved very much the minute he saw it. When he got home he called his mother.

"Hi Mom," said Robert. "Guess what, I just bought an engagement ring. I am going to propose to Lorrie."

"That is fantastic," said Robert's mother. "I love that girl."

"I am going to see her tomorrow night," said Robert. "I wonder, should I give it to her then? I am hesitant because I would like a happier location, like some kind of party."

"Robert honey," said his mother. "Can I make a suggestion?" "Of course," said Robert. "That's why I called you."

"I would suggest that you put it off until Saturday evening," said Robert's mother. "Tell her that you both are invited here for an evening dinner. Tell her something like I would like to see her again, that I would like to meet the new person she now is."

"That sounds great," said Robert. "Are you going to invite anyone else?"

"I'll see what I can do," said Robert's mother. "Trust me." After they hung up Robert spent the rest of the day thinking of what he could say in his proposal effort. Finally it was Friday evening. At six o'clock Robert picked up Lorrie.

"Hi honey," said Robert. "How are you tonight?"

"I'm fine," said Lorrie. "Where are we going for dinner?"

"I though you would like some home cooked Tilapia tonight," said Robert.

"That will be great," said Lorrie. "I loved the fish you cooked. After we eat we can see the movie we didn't get see completely Wednesday." "What do you mean completely," said Robert with laughter in his voice. "We didn't see any of it." Lorrie smiled happily. When they got to Robert house they went inside and Robert went directly to the kitchen. The fish was ready to cook. All he had to do is put in the oven and turn on the broiler button. After Robert said his prayer they started to eat.

"This is so good," said Lorrie. "I have missed the delicious food you cook."

"You are not so bad a cook yourself," said Robert. "I remember some of the delicious dinners you prepare for us. "Did you get some indication as to why you are such a great Italian dinner chef?"

"In a couple of the folders I reviewed and studied I found some evidence that my mother came from Italian background. How else would she have all the recipes that she had. By the way one of the things I found and brought with me is my mother's personal recipe book. I will be happy to cook some of them for you. I also learned that my mother passed away when I was a teenager."

"Did you learn anything," asked Robert, "about your father?"
"Not too much," saaid Lorrie. "The only thing that I can assume is that after my mother died and I was away to college that he moved to California and never looked back."

"By the way," asked Robert. "Are you free tomorrow night?"
"Yes," said Lorrie, "what do you have in mind?"

"My mother has invited us to dinner tomorrow night," answered Robert. "She says she want to meet the new Loretta."

"I would love that," said Lorrie. "They are like my new parents."
"You don't know the half of that," said Robert. Then trying to change the subject he added. "Now that we are finished eating let's go see that rest of the movie we didn't see last Wednesday. They both laughed at that statement. "We will have dessert after the movie. "I will wash the dishes after I take you home."

"Sounds like a good plan," said Lorrie. That evening they neither saw the movie nor had dessert. At midnight Robert took Lorrie home.

Saturday morning Robert slept until nine. He ate breakfast and went back to writing his novel. The new ideas he got was so intensifying that time flew by and he suddenly found out it was past noon. He ate a light lunch and went back to his novel. It was hard to write now, as Robert was thinking of what he was going to say that night. Soon it was time for Robert to pick up Lorrie.

"Hi," said Lorrie as she came out the door. She had been waiting just inside the door.

"Hi Lorrie," said Robert. "You look fantastic. I will be so proud to show you off."

"Thank you," said Lorrie, "what is going on?" "Nothing," said Robert. "Why do you ask?" "You look jollier then you usually do," said Lorrie. "I just have missed you," said Robert.

"You just saw me last night," said Lorrie.

"Well it is different now," said Robert. "I'm going to show you off to my parents. It is different because I'm going to tell them that you are parent's house at six thiirty. Robert knocked on the door. His mother answered the door.

"Hi Robert, Lorrie," said his mother. "Come on in." As they walked into the front room they were shocked at what they saw.

"Hi Daddy," said Liana as she hugged him. Before he could say another work Amy came and hugged him

"Hi Daddy." she said.

"Where did you guys come from," asked Robert, "and when did you guys get here?" Before they could answer his sister Teresa came and hugged him.

"Good to see you dear brother," said Teresa. "Hi Daddy," said Tommy. "Good to see you." "What are all of you doing here?" asked Robert.

"We thought it was a time to get all of our family together," said Roberts father as they hugged. "It's about time we all have a party together." They all hugged Lorrie and welcomed her to the party. The shock at seeing every one caused Robert to forget why they were all there. Finally he figured out that his mom had set this all up as an engagement party.

"Let's all sit at the dining room table," said Robert's mother. "The food is ready." As they all sat down Robert's Mom made a suggestion. "Let us make a toast to this occasion. Robert, do you want to make the first toast?"

"Yes I have a special toast to make, but first I have a question to ask," said Robert. He then asked Lorrie to stand. After she stood up he went down on one knee. "I would like to make this event very special. I would like to make this our engagement party. Lorrie I love you with all of my heart. Will you marry me?" Lorrie had tears in her eyes as she realizes what Robert was asking, and suddenly realized what the gathering was for. Now with full tears she barely got out the words.

"Yes I will marry you," she barely got out.

"Hurray" yelled out Robert's mother. "I want to make the first toast. "I wish that Robert and Lorrie have the best life and happiness they could have."

"Here, here, herre," yelled everyone. Robert then hugged Lorrie and gave her a very passionate kiss. The kiss lasted over a minute.They felt like they were up in heaven and they felt like they were alone. When they finally parted they noticed that Robert's mother was serving the meal. It was Cavatelli with a special tomato sauce. After they had finished eating, Robert's father put on some music. Most of the people there danced at least once. At about eight Robert's mother announced that dessert was being served. She then brought in a large cake. On the top if the cake were the words,'Happy engagement Robert and Lorrie.' The evening was a joy to everyone. It was after twelve when they all decided to end the party and go home. The farewell hugs they all got were memorial.

"Are you girls going to come home with me?" Robert asked of Liana and Amy.

I don't think I can," said Amy. "I am supposed to be at work tomorrow at twelve. I am going to be late as it is. I am going to leave right after church tomorrow. Your mother has been so kind to give us your old bed room. I am going to stay here tonight"

"Me too," said Liana. "I have a long way to go. Sorry Dad." Robert hardly remembered dropping off Lorrie and going home.

The next day Robert called Lorrie early in the morning.

"Do you want me to pick you up for church tomorrow?" he asked. "No I'll meet you in church," she said. "I just got up and I am going to be late if I don't hurry. I'll meet you in church."

"Will you come to my house after church?" assked Robert. "I have a nice piece of filet minion waiting for you."

I will follow you home after the service," said Lorrie. "How can I pass that up?" When she got to the church, the service had not started. She showed her ring to a young girl named Karan who she had met before when they knew her as Cathy. Soon half of the church were there viewing the ring and congratulating them. Just as the service was about to start, the pastoor came to see what the fuss was all about. When they told him he conngratulated them. He had remembered them as a couple since Robert brought her to his home. The pastor had known Robert since he became the church pastor. After the service some of the other church members followed them to the church exit. Ten miutes later they both arrived at Robert's house. Robert quickly got the grill heated up and soon had the steaks cooking. Lorrie wouldn't just sit and watch Robert cooking, so she went into the kitchen and prepared a salad. She knew her way around Roberts's refrigerator and freezer. She found some peas in the freezer and defrosted then in the microwave and then put them in a pan and started to cook them. When Robert came in from the grill which was outside in the patio he was surprised with all that Lorrie had done. They decided to eat under the umbrella in the patio.

"Where do we go from here, dear?" Asked Lorrie

"You know that my two daughters were here a few days ago for their spring vacation," said Robert. "We visited so many places that I can hardly remember them all. I was thinking that I could take you to a few that I liked the best and that I think you would also like."

"Give me an example of what you are talking about," said Lorrie "Well the first is Cedar Point Amusement Park," said Robert. We went on so many wonderful rides like the roller coaster."

"Yes I see what you mean," said Lorrie, "that reminds me of a desire I have. Remember when we went to the Cleveland Zoo that we had to leave early because we were invited to your mother's dinner. We didn't see some of the animals. I would like to go there first."

"That is fine with me," said Robert. "However we have a problem. When are you able to take a full day off? What days do you have available?"

"Yes I forgot that I now have a job," said Lorrie. "We will have to think about that."

"Well when will you be available?" asked Roberts, "and what evening will we be together?"

"I work until four thirty but don't leave until about five," said Lorrie. "I get home aboout five thirty. On Monday evening I do my weekly shopping. Tuesday evening is my clean up period.

Wednesday I can sometime get the day off. Thursday is my do everythingI haven't done earlier in the week. I guess what you are asking is, when can we be able to be together"

"I guess," said Robert, "from what you just said, is that I can only see you on Wednesday, Friday, Saturday, and Sunday after church. Is that what you are saying?"

"I'm sorry," said Lorrie, "but that is the time I have available." "What is up with Wednesday?" asked Robert.

"You know that the doctors that have offices in the building sent their patients down to the lab for different tests," said Lorrie. "Well doctors take off on Wednesday so they don't send patients down that day. However patient sometimes don't make it on Tuesday so they show up on Wednesday. And sometimes they come with test requests from doctors from other locations. Most of the time we only have one or two patients, so I can take off anyway"

"Then let's plan on this Wednesday to go to the zoo to see what we didn't see before," said Robert.

"Fine," said Lorrie. "How about picking me up at about ten Wednesday morning," said Lorrie. After dinner Robert put on a movie that Lorrie picked out from his collection of movies. Robert turned on the movie. They did not see any part of the movie. At about ten Robert took Lorrie home.

Monday morning Robert checked all the places that they could have the wedding reception. He found a place called Toodaro's Party Center that he was impressed with. On Tuesday he checked all the florists and bands. He was ready to discuss his finding with Lorrie to set a wedding date. Wednesday he picked up Lorrie at ten.

"Hi honey," said Robert as Lorrie opened the door.

"Hi fiancé," said Lorrie with a happy smile on her face. "Are you ready to go to the zoo?"

"I would like to make a change in our plans," said Robert. "Wednesday would be a better time to go to the Cedar Point. The reason I suggest the chaange is because if we go to the Zoo now, then we would want to go to CedarPoint on Saturday. Saturdays are very crowded at an amusement park. We would have to wait in long line and probably would not get on all the rides. Saturday would be a better time to go to the zoo."

"That is OK with me," said Lorrie. "I am in the mood for an adventure at an amusement park. Anyway you are the driver. I will go where ever you take me." About an hour later they entered the park. The parking lot was full.

"Look at the number of cars that are here," said Robert. "Imagine how many there would be here on Saturday." Inside they found that the lines for all the rides were pretty long.

"Let's go through all the game booths," said Lorrie. "Maybe later the lines will not be so long." They did go around the park visiting all the action booths. They tried the bow and arrow booth. Neither could hit the target. At the rifle booth Lorrie did hit one of the targets.

That was great," said Robert. "Now you will have a souvenir to take home with you." Lorrie chose a cute little doll. Half way through the park they stopped for a hamburger. Afterwards they continued through the rest of the booths. At about five in the afternoon they started to go on the rides. The lines were much shorter at that time. Robert and Lorrie went on most of the rides. Lorrie insisted that Robert ride with her. He couldn't refuse her. At about seven they left the park and stopped at Olive Garden for dinner. Robert explained to her what he had researched for their wedding. She liked the information he gave her. She said she wanted to research his choices further. After that Robert took Lorrie home and he went home. They were both very tired.

Thursday they both were very busy. Robert had many bills to take care of and receiving the check book statement from the bank, he had to check it against his check book. Lorrie had to work and returning home she decided to wash her clothes. Friday Robert picked Lorrie up at six and they went to Red Loobster for dinner. Lorrie had a desire for scrimp.

"I have reviewed the information you gave me," said Lorrie. I liked it. I contacted Todaro's Party Center and made reservations for May tenth. They did not have anything sooner. The lady I talked with asked us togo see her to pick out invitation cards. We will have to do that. I also called the florist and two bands. The lady from Todaro's recommended a band they have used many times. I called and I liked the one they recommended better. I hope you agree with all that I've done so far."

"I think you are doing as fine job," said Robert. "I agree with all that you have done. However, I or you should keep in touch with Todaro's in case there is a cancelation."

I have already handled that," said Lorrie. "I asked them to let me know if there was a cancellation."

"I guess you have everything covered," said Robert. After dinner they went to Roberts home to see the movie that they liked but didn't get to see. They didn't see it that evening either. Saturday at ten Robert arrived at Lorrie's house. When she opened the door Robert spoke out.

"Hello fiancé," said Robert beating her to the punch. How are you today? Are you ready to go to the zoo?"

"I would like to make a change to that plan," said Lorrie. "It is such a beautiful day, with low humility, great temperature, and great green growth around. It will probably be the last of the sweet fall days." "What do you want to do?" asked Robert being surprised by her comments.

"I think it will be a nice day to have a picnic," said Lorrie.o

"Are we ready to have a picnic?" asked Robert. "I don't have a blanket or any food for a picnic."

"You of little faith," said Lorrie. "I have everything we need." She then pulled out a large picnic basket full of food. She also pulled out a large blanket.

"Well let's go," said Robert. "I know the exact place for a great picnic. I will take you to Sand Run Metropolitan Park." Robert put everything in his car and a few minutes later they arrived at the park. They walked through the woods until they came to a small clearing that was covered with green grass. They laid the blanket under a heavy leaved tree and laid the picnic basket on it.

"I think it is a little too early to eat so let's just sit here and watch the wind gently brush the tree leaves," said Lorrie.

"You know," said Robert. "I was here with my daughters just a few days ago. I spent most of the time watching them throw a baseball around. They were very good at throwing the ball and catching it. They were like two baseball players." Lorrie decided to lie down on the blanket. Robert lied down next to her and put his arm around her.

They laid there for over an hour in each other arms. Finally they decided to eat lunch. Lorrie had brought two Tuna Fish sandwiches, Two Turkey Breast sandwiches, two Italian salami sandwiches and two baloney sandwiches. Robert chose a tuna sandwich.

"I thought you would pick that sandwich," said Lorrie. "You love fish. I'm going have a Turkey sandwich."

"Why do you have so many sandwiches?" said Robert. "Were you trying to guess what I would eat?"

"I think that with all this fresh air you may want more than one sandwich and a different kind for your second sandwich." Lorrie was right. Robert chose an Italian salami sandwich for his second. After they finish the sandwiches Lorrie had two different desserts.

"We still have four sandwiches left," said Robert. "What is your plan for them?"

"What I would suggest," said Lorrie, "is that we put them in your car and take a nice hike through the woods. There is a niice path just on the other side of this area. After we are tired of seeing all that there is to see, I think it will be around five o'clock, we then can take out the picnic basket and have dinner."

"You have this whole picnic well planned," said Robert. "It does sound like a good plan so let's get started." They then walked back to the car and put away the picnic basket. They then found the path and stared the walk through the wooods. After walking for about ten miutes they came to a small stream. They walked the path which led down the edge of the stream. The beauty of the landscape around the stream was amazing. They had no idea that the area would be so enjoyable to see. Further downstream they came to a rocky place. The stream was like a hundred small waterfalls. The land did go up as they walked along the shore. Finally they got to the end which ran under a bridge that was on a small country road. The way back was just as delightful. They got back to the car at about a quarter to six. They didn't bother to lay out the blanket. They ate dinner sitting in the car. After eating they drove to Robert's house. This time they did watch the movie. They were too tired to do anything else.

Sunday they met at church. After the service they drove to McDonalds for a hamburger. They didn't want to eat too much because Lorrie had invited Robert to a special dinner Sunday night. They left the church using Robert's car. They left Lorrie's car in the church parking lot. After lunch they drove to the Stan Hywet Tudor Manor. They walked through the 65 room manor. However, they enjoyed the Stan Hywet gardens more than the house. Lorrie was wowed by it all.

"What is this?" asked Lorrie, "Is this a castle of an American President?"

"It was the house of the president of the company that invented the rubber that is used in Goodyear's tires," informed Robert. "Since that historic time it became too expensive for anyone to live here. So it became a historic monument." After reviewing the grounds they left and went to church to retrieve Lorrie's car. From there they went to Lorrie's house. Lorrie went into the kitchen which was just behind the living room. There was a hallway in the left of the entrrance to the kitchen. Down the hall way was the bathroom and two bedrooms. There was no dining room or family room. Robert went into the living room where there was a television. He stayed there watching the news program while Lorrie cooked him the special dinner. About fifteen miutes later Lorrie called Robert into the kitchen. She had cooked Sausage casserole.

"How in the world did yoou cook this in just a few miutes?" asked

Robert. "I know when my mother cooked sausage, and it was seldom, it took about an hour."

"I did it all this morning," said Lorrie. "I got up early. I placed the sausage, the potatoes and all the other ingredients in the baking pan with the tomato sauce, covered it and put it in the oven. I set the oven timer to turn on at eleven o'clock and to shut off at twelve o'clock. That is why it is ready to eat now. That is one of the few things that I remember my mother teaching me."

"Wow," said Robert as he as he looked in the pan. "It looks so delicious. It also smells so wonderful"

"I'm glad you like it," said Lorrie. "I think it come out better than usual. I think it is because I used Sicilian sausage. The secret is that

I cooked the sausage a little last night so that it would cook quicker. Covering it keeps the moisture inside the sausage." Lorrie then served the food.

"It is fantastic," said Robert as he helped himself to another serving. After they finished eating Lorrie brought out a Razzleberry Pie. Robert couldn't tell what berries were in it but it was delicious. All the food was served with coffee. After dinner they sat and watched a movie. It was so interesting that they did watch most of it. Robert always managed to keep his romance to hugging and kissing. He never forgot that he was a Born-again Christian.

Monday and Tuesday went by as usual. Lorrie did her shopping on Monday evenings and cleaned her house on Tuesday. Wednesday at ten Robert presented himself at Lorrie's door.

"Good morning there, love of my live," said Robert. "Are you ready to tour the zoo?"

"I would like to make a change to our plan," said Lorrie. "Not again," said Robert. "What is it this time?"

"I think we should go to Todaro's to confirm our reservation date," said Lorrie. "And while we are there, let's pick an invitation card."

"I think that you are right," said Robert. "We should take care of that first. We could then have lunch and then go to the zoo. I think we will have plenty of time tosee all that we didn't see the last time." "It only took them a few minutes to get to Todaro's. When  they walked in they approached the entrance desk.

"Good Morning," said Robert. "We are Robert Bensen and Loretta James. We are here to confirm our reservation and pick and order our invitation cards."

Yes," said the young man behind to entrance desk. That is Nancy's job. Please step in the office on your left there and sit at the table across from her desk." Robert and Lorrie did as asked and sat down on the table chairs so that they sat across from the desk. They barely sat down when a young woman came in and sat at the desk.

"Good Morning," she said. "It's so nice to meet you. I am Nancy Rose. I take it that you are Robert Bensen and Loretta James. What can I do for you today?"

"We are here to confirm our reservation and to choose and order our invitation cards." said Robert. Nancy opened the drawer of her desk and pulled out a note book.

"I see that you have asked for reservation on May the tenth of next spring," said Nancy. "You have also made reservation for the band and the florist. I will need a deposit for your reservation here at Todaro's and a deposit for the band. I suggest you go to the florist about two months before your wedding and chose you flowers. He will want full payment at that time." After Robert agreed Nancy brought out several samples of invitation cards. She spread the cards on the table. Lorrie immediately fell in love with one of the samples.

"This is so beautiful," said Lorrie. "This is the one I want." "Let's sit here and figure how many we want," said Robert. They sat and started to count all the people they wanted to invite. First they named Lorrie's. There weren't very many. They were primarily a few from work. Robert had a lot more. After adding them all up they added twenty percent more just to be safe. When they were all done Nancy summed up the total and gave it to Robert. Robert wrote a check for the amount asked by Nancy. Nancy then put the check away and wished them a beautiful day. They left Todaro's and went directly to the zoo. When they walked throughthe monkey cage Lorrie grabbed Robert by the arm.

"Don't try to go into the monkey cage," said Lorrie smiling. "Very funny," said Robert also smiling. They walked quickly through area they had already seen the last time they were there. They then concentrated on the area they had never seen. That area included the larger animals like the giraffe which Lorrie was most impressed with. She couldn't get over how it could exist with such a long neck. It was about nine thirty when they left and on the way home  they stopped at Olive Garden for a large dinner. It was large because they had missed lunch. After they ate, they were too full to do anything so Robert took Lorrie home.

The next day was Monday. Robert slept late and got up at about eleven. He ate an early lunch and then went back to working on his book. At about six he ate his dinner and then went back to writing his book. He was getting to a very exciting part of his book when the doorbell rang. Robert answered the door.

"Lorrie," he yelled out being surprised at seeing her. "I thought this was the day you went grocery shopping."

"It is," said Lorrie. "However I need your help. You see I want to learn how to cook a couple of the nice meals that you cook. I want you to come with me and help me pick the items I need to cook them."

"Which items, asked Robert, "do you want to cook?"

I want to learn how to cook three of your fantastic dinners. First I want to learn how to cook your Tilapia fish. Next I want to learn how you cook Baby Back Ribs. Which type do you buy and how do you cook them so the meat is so tender that it just falls off the bone, and last I want to know how you cook Cavatelli with Pork Neck Bones."

"The secret with Tilapia is the sauce I put on them and that I broil them instead of grilling them," said Robert. "The ribs I cut them so that they include two bones. I then wrap them in aluminum foil and bake them for two hours. After that I open the foil so that the top of the ribs are showing and I coat them with barbecue sauce. I then broil them for five miutes until they have anice brown coat and then take them out."

"That's enough,," said Lorrie you will have to show me, one at a time how to cook them. I can't remember what you just described. Right now I need you to come with me and pick out all the items that you will need for each meal as if you were buying them for yourself."

"All right," said Robert. "I'll drive. They got into Robert's car and drove down Bancroft to Elgin Drive and turn right on Elgin and drove down to Cleveland Massillon Road. Robert drove up to the traffic light driving on to the left turning lane. He suddenly was curious of the black car that drove along side of them. He looked over to see who it was when he saw a rifle sticking out of the window. Without thinking, he grabbed Lorrie by the back of her neck and shoved her down under the glove compartment and laid himself on top of her. The pain he suddenly felt made him lose consciousness. Lorrie hearing the shots and feeling Robert on top of her realized what was happening. She reached for her purse which was between her legs and got her cell phone. She dialed 911.

"Help," she yelled, "Someone is shooting at us." She then told them where she was. However before she could shut off her phone she heard the siren of a police car. Someone else had called the police. Soon someone opened her door and pulled Robert off of her.

"Are you OK," asked one the officers that helped her out of the car.

"How is Robert?" she said. "Please take care of him." Then she kept repeating, "Oh Jesus, help us Jesus," She was not concerned for her health. She was concerned for Robert. She could not answeer the police man because all she could think of was Robert's condition, and the possibility that she could lose him. The next thing she became aware of was that she was in an ambulance with Robert. "How is Robert?" she asked the man that was taking care of them in the ambulance.

"We will not know until he is checked by the doctor at the hospital," said the young man. "All I can tell you at this time is that he is still alive. We are trying to control his bleeding." A few minutes later they arrived at Akron General Hospital. Lorrie was lead to a hospital bed.

"I am Nurse Christa," said the nurse that helped her into the room. "The doctor will be with you soon."

"I don't really need a doctor," said Lorrie. "I'm OK. I am worried about my fiancé. Can you tell me how he is?"

He is down in surgery," said the nurse. "The ambulance nurse took good care of him." Officer Bill who had been in another part of the hospital taking care of another case finally walked into the room where Lorrie was.

"Hi Lorrie," he said. "How are you? Are you alright?"

"I fine," said Lorrie. "I'm so worried about Robert. I can't lose him. He is all of my life. "I don't remember any other life."

"I'm sure that he will be fine," said Bill. "He is a Born Again Christian. God will take care of him. God needs him here on earth for a long time." Slowly Bill got Lorrie relaxed and they spent the next couple of hours talking. Lorrie told Bill her whole story from the time Robert dropped her off at Indiana to the time of the accident. While they were still talking, the doctor walked into the room.

"Hello Cathy," said the doctor. "Or I guess you real name now is Loretta. How are you? Do you remember me? I'm Doctor Brenner. I took care of you when you were here with the head injury."

"Oh yes," said Lorrie. "Of course I remember you. You and Nurse Christa were the only persons I knew except for Officer Robert Bensen. Oh doctor how is Robert? I am so worried about him."

He is going to be fine," said the doctor. "We had to operate and remove the bullet that was inside by his lung. It was necesssary not only to remove the bullet but also to stop the bleeding. All though, thanks to the ambulance crew, who did a great job in stopping the bleeding. The other bullet was parallel to his body. It entered his back and came out his shoulder. It apparently hit him after he had laid down over you."

"When can we see him?" asked Lorrie.

"He is in the recovery room," said the doctor. "He will be out in about two hours; however he will not be awake until morning if even then."

"When will he be able to go home," asked Lorrie.

"It will take at least a couple of days," responded the doctor. We have to make sure his bleeding doesn't come back. But for now I would like to give you a complete examination.

"I'm feeling fine," said Lorrie. "Is it necessary?"

"Yes," said the doctor. "It is required by all insurance companies. It is required to prevent a law suit later."

"I'll wait outside," said Bill as he left. The examination did not take long. When he was done he said he would see her tomorrow because he was finished for the day. Bill came in after the doctor left.

"I am leaving also," he said as he started to leave. "It is past ten o'clock. I will see you in the morning."

It was after twelve o'clock when the nurse came in and told Lorrie that Robert had been moved to his own room. Lorrie quickly went to Robert's room. She was surprised to see a police man sitting in front of the room.

"What are you doing here?" asked Lorrie.

"I am the guard to watch that no one comes in here except the ones that are approved by the doctor." When she walked into the room she saw that Robert was lying on his good side. His hand was sticking out in front of him. Lorrie pulled the chair with the soft pillows next to his bed and sat down next to him. After about an hour, holding Robert's hand, Lorrie fell asleep. In the morning Lorrie was awakened by Nurse Christa who had just come to work.

"Hi Lorrie," she said, as Lorrie woke from the noise the nurse made. "How are you today? I see you have been here all night. You are lucky. They usually have visitors leave at eight o'clock."

"I guess I am not a visitor since I was examined by the attending doctor."

"Has the patient opened his eyes yet this morning or moved at all?" asked the nurse.

"No," said Lorrie, "not that I know of. But I have been asleep all night." It was a little after one in the afternoon when Robert began to move.

"Hi honey," said Lorrie as soon as his eyes opened. Robert tried to move but stopped due to the pain. It was several minutes before Robert could respond.

"Hi Lorrie," he said. "Are you alright?" "I'm fine," said Lorrie, "how do you feel?"

"I feel like I have been run over by a truck," said Robert. Just as he finished talking the doctor came in.

"Hi," he said to them. "How is my patient this morning? Don't answer I hear your comment as I walked in. I'm sorry I'm late but I worked several hours overtime yesterday." The doctor turned Robert to a more comfortable position. He then did a full examination. "I think that he is healing pretty well. Looks like the blood leakage as stopped."

"How soon can I go home?" asked Robert.

"I think you have to stay about two more days," said the doctor. Soon after the doctor left, Lorrie bent over and kissed Robert with a long lasting kiss. They talked the rest of the morning telling each other how much they loved each other and how frightened they were about each other's health. At about twelve the nurse came in with a special hospital dish and fed Robert. Lorrie went down to the main floor where there was a restaurant. She had a light lunch and went back upstairs. Soon after she got back, Bill walked in.

"How are you doing Robert?" asked Bill "I've had better days," said Robert.

"And how are you holding up Lorrie?" asked Bill.

I am somewhat relieved," said Lorrie. "I was so worried about Robert that I didn't even think of myself."

"I didn't come in this morning because I have started working on finding the one who tried to kill you," said Bill. "I have started with Amy's family and the families of the two you put in jail. However you got to get well because I need your help. There are so many possibilities with all the people you have put in jail."

"Well it is a good idea to check Amy's background," said Robert. "I don't think you will find anything but at least we could get that possibility out of the way."

"Your right," said Bill. "I could not find any relatives of Lorrie that would have a reason to want you dead. I am in the process of checking the fellow and his girlfriend that you put into jail. I plan on going to Columbus State Prison and talking with them. "I will see you tonight," said Bill as he was leaving. Lorrie then pulled herself next to Robert.

"Listen Lorrie," said Robert. "We have to talk."

"What do you have in mind?" asked Lorrie. "I am fine."

"I think you can stay here until tonight," said Robert, "but after that I don't think we should see each other."

"Are you trying to dump me," said Lorrie before he could finish. She had a very hurt look on her face.

"You didn't let me finish," said Robert. "I love you more than my life. What I was saying is that we should not be together until we find out who is trying to kill me. This last time we lucked out and you didn't get hurt. I don't want you to be an innocent bystander and get hurt if the person trying to kill me tries again. Please. You can go back to work and in the evening just spend the time praying that we soon catch the shooter."

"I'm willing to take the chance," said Lorrie.

"I am not," said Robert. "Besides, I will be distracted from finding the shooter spending the time to protect you."

"If that is what you want so be it," said Lorrie. "Let's not waste the little time we will have together." She then walked to the room door and called the police officer that was protecting the room. Officer, please don't let anyone in here except the doctor. Not even the nurse is to disturb us. I will let her know when we need anything. When she is bringing dinner for Robert tell her to knock on the door before entering."

"As you wish said the officer who understood better than Lorrie realized. Lorrie then shut the door and went to Robert. Robert never had so many kisses before in his life.

# CHAPTER SEVEN

# THE DIFFICULT ROAD TO ROMANCE

THE NEXT TWO DAYS went by slowly. Robert was released from the hospital. He got home about four thirty. He waited about a half hour and then he called Lorrie. She had just gotten home. Her work day ended at four thirty.

"Hi sweet heart," said Robert. "I see that you are home safely. I was released from the hospital and I just got home. I'm fine and I'm going to start looking for the shooter. The sooner I find him the sooner we can be together."

"Hi honey," said Lorrie. "I guess a few minutes on the phone are all we will have until you solve this case." They did talk for a few miutes and too soon they decided that they had to hang up.

The next morning Robert was at the police station. He went directly to Bill's office.

"Hi Bill," said Robert as he went in and sat down across from Bill's desk. What have you found out so far?"

"I have all the people that could have possibly known Amy. The two people that tried to steal all her money are in jail. I talked with them and they are very sorry in what they did. I found some distant cousins of Amy, but I found that they were out of state and they were all at work when you got shot. So what I'm saying is that I have nothing about her. Today I have been checking all the  old assignment you had with the same results."

"I am not surprised," said Robert. "We have to concentrate on the latest assignments, namely the Casta family and the Bladen family."

"Let's investigate the Casta family first," said Bill. "I have already started on that one."

"What have you gotten so far?" asked Robert.

"I have contacted George's sister, Sophia, his mother Martha, and his father Joseph. They all claimed that he was disinherited years ago. I checked their place of employment and they were all at work on the day you were shot."

"I checked Annie's family when we first investigated the murder," said Robert, "and they are all clean. I also checked John's family and they are all happy of the results and they were all at work when I was shot. So I think that part is a dead end.

"All we have left is the rest of George's family" said Bill.

"Well, why don't you check for any relatives of George's wife Vera and I will check for relatives of Vera's brother-in-law Vincent."

"Sounds like a good plan," said Bill, "and you don't know how happy I am that you are here to help. Please feel free to make any suggestion."

"I'm glad I could help," said Robert. "We have to find this guy quickly." From that moment on both spent most of the day on computers and telephones. Finally Bill interrupted Robert.

"I have been trying to contact Vera's sister Helen, but I'm told that her phone is not in service," said Bill, "I wonder if she is having money problems."

"Well," said Robert, "It is after four thirty so why don't we drive to her house and see what her problem is. We could use the time to relax anyway."

"Sounds like a good idea," said Bill "Let's go." It only took a few minutes and they were at her house. Bill knocked on the door. A young woman came to the door.

"How can I help you?" she asked.

"We are looking for Helen Braden," said Robert. "Who are you?" "I live here," said the woman. "We just bought this house from someone named Braden."

"I'm sorry we bothered you," said Bill. They both went back to Bill's car.

"I'm glad we took your car," said Robert. "Having a police car there kept her from being frightened."

"You know," said Bill. "As long as we are out, let's stop at Vera's house. "She can tell us what happened to Helen."

"Let me give her a call and get permission to see her," said Robert. "That's a good Idea," said Bill. "Do you have her phone number?" Robert didn't answer. He just got his phone out and made the call. He got permission and Bill drove to her house.

Hi, come on in," said Vera when they got there. "What do I owe for the honor of this visit?" she asked.

"Well we are talking to everyone who knows Robert," said Bill. "Someone tried to kill him. He got shoot in the shoulder few days ago. As you can see he is well now but we have to find who did this."

"How can I help?" asked Vera.

"Mainly what we wouldlike to know is what happened to your sister Helen," said Robeert. "We found out that she sold her home and disappeared."

"Yes," said Vera with a smile on her face. "She is with her husband in Columbus. Vincent, due to your testimony that it was an accident and self-defense at worse, was released on probation. He is free as long as he stays in Columbus and reports to the probation officer once a week. Helen, with all her experience and background, had no trouble finding a job. Vincent got a job as a janitor in a small business building. They are happier than they have ever been. They would have no reason to hurt you Officer Robert."

"I think we have all that we need," said Bill. "Thank you for your time."

"Tell your sister that we wish her well," said Robert as they left. When in the car Robert turned to Bill.

"Well it looks like that one is a dead end also," said Bill.

"It will be the first crime we have not solved," said Robert, "and the most important. Let's go see the Captain and see what he says."

"I don't know if he is still there," said Bill. "He does work late sometimes." From Vera's house they went directly to the police station. They had planned on going to get something to eat so they skipped that and went directly to see if the Captain was there.

Fortunately he was in his office. They walked right in and declared their problem.

"We have come up with zero success," said Bill.

"Where have you guys been," said the Captain, "I know why you are not successful. It happened that Robert was not the target. The target was Loretta James."

"What makes you think that?" asked Robert with deep concern in his face.

"Because the shooter was successful," said the Captain. "I sent two officers to the Fairlawn Mall where the shooting took place. They called an ambulance and are taking Loretta to the Akron General Hospital. She had multiple wounds." Robert did not hesitate to ask any more questions He asked Bill for the key to the police car.

Nonsense," said Bill. "I can't let you drive. Come I will take you." They got into the police car and at full speed and the siren at full volume they raced to the hospital. When they got there they pulled up to the emergence entrance were Bill could park his car right up to the entrance door. They quickly went inside. Bill showed his police badge and asked where the wounded lady was taken. She told them she was on the third floor. They rushed there and were met by the nurse.

"Where do you have the wounded woman that was brought up here?" asked Robert.

"She will be in room 312 when she comes up from surgery. She was in very bad shape I understand. She died on the way here but a good ambulance nurse brought her back to life. She had lost too much blood. They had to give her a transfusion before they could operate. They had to remove two bullets and stop the bleeding. I will let you know when she will be brought up to her room. There is an officer watching her room. He came with them and can tell you more." Robert walked to the room.

"Hi Ralph," said Robert recognizing the officer. "What are you doing here?"

"I'm here to see that no one except the Doctor and the doctor approved nurse can come in."

"I understand that you were first on the crime scene and that you came in the ambulance," said Robert. "Tell me all that you know. How bad was Lorrie hurt?"

"Her heart actually stopped on the way here. An ambulance fellow brought her back to life. She had two bullets in her. One looked like it was in the chest and the other in the shoulder. I am praying that she will be alright." That snapped Robert to the present situation. He walked into the room and knelt down next to the bed and started to pray. He had to trust in the Lord. After about ten minutes he was interrupted by Bill.

"Are you all right?" asked Bill. "I was worried about you. I didn't know where you went. Ralph told me that you came into the room."

"I had to come somewhere alone to pray. The Lord has always answered my prayers." They went out and sat in the waiting room. Robert continued to pray silently. Bill spent the time reading the magazines that were available there in the waiting room. It was over two hours later that the doctor walked into the waiting room. Robert recognized him right away.

"Hi doctor Brenner," said Robert. "I'm glad it is you that is taking care of Lorrie. How is she?"

"She is doing better," said the doctor. "We had to remove two bullets from her body. One bullet went into the shoulder. That one was not a problem. The one that has us worried is the one that entered her chest. It just scratched the heart, but did damage to the end of her lung. That is why we have her on oxygen. We hope her lung will heal without further bleeding. We have brought her up to her room. However we are keeping her sedated. We want her to get a lot of rest. She will not awake for two days providing there will be no problem showing up. So how are you? Mrs. James and you are making a habit of coming here." "We will try to stop doing that," said Robert. "Will it be alright if

I stay here all night? I want to be here in case she has a problem." "Yes you may," said the doctor. "We have an evening doctor who will look into her every hour and a nurse that check her ever ten miutes.

If you want my opinion, she will be alright. She is too strong and healthy to submit to her problem." After saying that, the doctor left.

"Listen Robert," said Bill. "I am going to leave. I won't come here early because I want to start looking into Loretta's families. I will come here in the evening after dinner. Good bye for now." Bill then left. Robert went into the Lorrie's hospital room pulled a chair next to her bed. He grabbed her hand and holding her hand he soon fell asleep. The nurse came in several times during the night to check the equipment that was hooked up to Lorrie, but she was careful not to wake up Robert.

It was early in the morning when Doctor Brenner came in to check on Lorrie that Robert woke up.

"Hi doc," said Robert. "HHow is your patient doing?"

"From what I see this morning she is going to be fine," said the doctor. "I will know moore after I giveher a complete checkup." Robert then left the room annd went out to the waiting room. There he saw Nurse Christa

"Hi Christa," said Robert. "How are you this morning?"

"I'm fine thank you," said Christa. "I see that Loretta is doing much better. You guys are here so often I think you should move in here." Robert smiled as Christa went on with her job down the hall. Robert sat down and grabbed a magazine. A few minutes later the doctor came out.

"You can go back in there again," said the doctor. "How is she doing doc?"

"She is doing better than I expected," said the doctor. "Her heart beat is back to normal, her blood pressure is normal and she is breathing on her own. I think we will let her come to this afternoon."

"I'll be here," said Robert. He then went back to the room and sat down next to the bed and grabbed Lorrie's hand. It was late in the afternoon that Bill came in.

"Hi Robert," said Bill. "How is Lorrie doing?"

She had improved fantastically," said Robert. "I think that she will be back to normal in a few days. What have you found out?" Before Bill could answer they heard Lorrie moaning.

"Lorrie honey," said Robert. "Wake up honey. I want to talk with you."

"Hi Robert," said Lorrie just opening her eyes, "where are we?" "Sweetheart," said Robert. "You are in the hospital. You have been shot. However, you are going to be alright." Lorrie tried to move. "Ouch," she said moving back to where she was. "My shoulder hurt," she said with another ouch coming out of her. "Was I shot in the shoulder?"

"You were shot in the shoulder and the chest. You had surgery and all is going to be alright."

"Hi Bill," said Lorrie becoming aware that Bill was there. "Do you know who it was that shot me?"

"Not yet," said Bill. "I'm working on it."

"What have you found out so far?" asked Robert.

"I have looked up all of the relatives that Lorrie has," started Bill. "I found that she has a father and a couple of distance cousins. I found no other relatives."

"Did you check on the whereabouts of these?"

"Yes," said Bill. "They all were accounted for at the time of the shooting. Her father is in Los Angeles and her cousins are in Arizona. They were all at work. Can I see you outside for a minute Robert?"

"You have something that you don't want me to hear," said Lorrie kidding Bill.

"It's another business that you don't have to be involved in." After Robert and Bill got outside, out of the hearing of Lorrie, Robert spoke first.

"What is the problem?" he asked.

"I just want you to agree with what I want to do," said Bill. "We are at a dead end with Lorrie's family. There is that news reporter Joan that comes into our office on every Wednesday that you know well. I would like to let it slip that Lorrie had passed away. Then I  will pretend that I was not aware that she was in hearing range, I'll then beg her to print that she was still alive in the hospital. I will tell her that we didn't want the killer to know that he had succeeded. You know her. She will print that she had passed away. I think that the person who shot her wants some of her inheritance, that way he will come forward to get some of the inheritance. I can't think of any other reason that anyone would want her dead. There must be someone of her relatives that I missed."

"Sounds like a great plan," said Robert. "Let's do it." They then walked into Lorrie's hospital room.

"I don't understand what is going on," said Lorrie. "Have you found who was trying to kill me?"

"I have checked all of your relative" said Bill, "But could not find anyone who would want you dead."

"Have you checked my huusband's family," asked Lorrie. "He must have had a family. I'm sorry but I still don't remember anyone in my past."

"Dear Lord," said Robert."We completely forgot that you had a husband in your past life. That is your next job Bill. Go check it out."

"I will get right on it," said Bill. He then said goodbye and left. "It was two days later that Bill came back to the hospital.

"Hi Robert," said Bill. "How is Lorrie? I see that she is not in her bed. Is something wrong?"

She is fine," said Robert. "They have her in the lab to do a final check of her vital organs. The doctor is considering letting her go home. So what have you come up with?"

"I found that Lorrie's husband, Doctor Ronald James, had a brother named Carl James who was married to a woman named Barbara. They had a son named Eric. The brother Carl passed away a year before Ronald died. The two brothers had a fight and the two families didn't associate for years. Carl's wife Barbara is very ill and needs surgery very badly. However they could not afford it. The son Eric just got out of jail for robbery so I think he is the main suspect."

"How did you make out with the newspaper girl Joan?"

"I walked past her and pretended that I didn't see her sitting by the door. I reported that Lorrie had died. Joan then got up and asked "did she die?" I begged her not to print it. I told her why and she said that she would think about it. Of course she printed it. I made sure that a copy went to Indiana.

"How do you plan on drawing the suspect out?" asked Robert. "The Captain and I have a plan," continued Bill. "We have announced that the funeral would take place this Friday and that the reading of the will be being held the day before in the funeral parlor office. We think that will bring our suspect out to claim some of the inheritance." Just then the doctor brought Lorrie back to her room. She was walking with a cane.

"Everything is fine," announced the doctor. She can go home on Thursday."

On Thursday Robert brought Lorrie to her house. He had a nurse there waiting for them.

"I have hired a nurse to take care of you for a few days" said Robert.

"I don't think it is necessary" said Lorrie but I have to get used to you being the boss," said Lorrie kidding him. Her laughter told Robert that she was kidding.

"Look honey I have to go and get informed to what is going on. I'll be back for dinner."

"Before you go," said Lorrie, "there is something I have to tell you. I hope you will forgive me for not telling you sooner.

"What's the problem?" asked Robert.

"While you were looking for the one that shot you I was home evenings all alone. One day the phone rang and it was Nancy from Todaro's. She told me that they had a cancellation. It is for September twelve. I then with her help got the florist and the musicians all arranged for the wedding. I also call the hotel at Niagara Falls and got reservation for a week after the wedding. So everything has been taken care of. What do you think?"

"Wow," said Robert. "That is only three months away. What about the invitation cards. Will they have the wrong date?"

"I called them also," said Lorrie. "They had not started the cards. They had a whole year to do it. I therefore had them change the date and they are starting to print it right away."

"Sounds great," said Robert. "I agree with all that you have done." "You don't think that September is too soon?" asked Lorrie.

"If it was possible for us to marry today," said Roberrt, "it would not have been too soon."

Before they knew it, it was Friday. Bill and Robert set up the reading of the will in the funeral parlor. At about two in the afternoon, a young man showed up.

"May I ask you how you are related to the deceased?" asked Bill "My name is Eric James," said the young man. "The deceased lady is my aunt Loretta James."

"Can you tell me why you are here?" asked Bill.

"My mother is very ill. She needs a surgery badly. I was hoping that my mother was in Aunt Lorrie's will. If it isn't I would like to apply for some of the inheritance." While they were talking, Robert walked out of the room. He already had a search warrant from the judge to search his car. He found it in the parking lot. It was the black foreign car he had seen when he was shoot. With the tools he had he opened the car. In the glove compartment he found the bill from the Hilton Hotel where he apparently stayed. In the trunk he found a rifle. He then got into his car and drove to the police lab. They immediately checked to see if the rifle was the one that had fired the bullets they retrieved from Robert and Lorrie. While he was waiting for the answer he called the Hilton Hotel. From them he found that Eric had been at the hotel for over two months. Soon the test results returned. The results found that the rifle was the gun that shot Robert and Lorrie. Robert then sent two police to pick up Eric. He then went to pick up Lorrie. He figured that she would like to face the man who tried to kill her.

At the Funeral Parlor, Eric got nervous.

"What is happening?" Erick asked Bill. "Am I the only relative? Where is the fellow that is going to read the will?"

"I think he is on his way," said Bill. "He is a little late and you are a little early." Just then the two police officers arrived.

"Is Eric James here?" One of the officers asked.

"I am Eric James," said Eric. "What do you want from me?" "We would like you to come with us," said the officer.

"I would like to stay her for the reading of the will," said Eric. "The will is to be discussed at the station," said the officer. "Since you are the only relative it will all take place at the station. The captain also would like to ask you question about your relationship with Loretta James."

"I will follow you in my car," said Eric.

"I'm sorry," said the officer. "We are to bring you directly to the captain.

"What about my car?" asked Eric, "What will happen to it?" "Give us the keys and we will see that it is brought to the station."

Seeing that he had no other alternative he went with the officers in the police car. At the station Eric was brought into the interrogation room. Soon the Captain walked into the room. With him were two other gentlemen.

"I am Captain Wilson," said the Captain, "and this on my right is Attorney Brian Edwin. And the other is Attorney Mark Douglas." The Captain did not tell Eric that Mark was also the Court Prosecutor. "I understand that you are the son of Carl James who is the brother of Loretta's husband Ronald James. Is that correct?"

"Yes," said Eric, "that is correct."

"Do you have any identification," asked the Captain.

"Yes," said Eric handing him his driver's license. The Captain handed it to the secretary.

"Have it checked for the finger prints," said the captain. "Isn't that taking this to extremes?" said Eric.

"We have to be sure that this is really you," said the Captain. A few miutes later the secretary came back and handed the driver's license back to Eric. She then looked at the captain.

"Yes," is all that she said and then left. In the meantime Robert and Lorrie came and stood just outside the room just listening to the conversations. They were not in sight of the people in the interrogation room.

"Mark," said the Captain. "Why don't you take over from here?" Mark walked out of the room and came back carrying a rifle.

"Is this your rifle," asked Mark of Eric.

"I don't have a rifle," said Eric. "Where did you find that one?" "I found it in the trunk of your car," said Mark. "Don't get that illegal look on your face, because I have a search warrant. I also have all the finger prints on the gun and from your driver's license. They all match. Our lab has also found the bullets that we got from Officer Bensen and Loretta James came from this gun." Eric got tears in his eyes. He realized that he was in serious trouble.

"What are you going to do to me?" he asked

"I am the court prosecutor," said Mark. "I will arrest you and charge you with a crime. What I charge you with will depend on you.

"What do you want me to do?" asked Eric now in full tears. "Start from the beginning and tell me why you did what you did," said Mark. "I promise you that if you tell the truth and confess your action that I will be easier on you."

"I originally came here to ask Aunt Lorrie for monetary help," started Eric. He had decided that to confess was the best thing to do. Somehow he trusted Mark. "The money was for my mother who needs an operation badly. Then I found out that she was going to get married. I realized that any money she had would go to her new husband. I had to get rid of her before she got married. I didn't mean to hurt the fellow in the car with Aunt Lorrie. He saw me and jumped in front of her. Later I found out where Aunt Lorrie lived and I followed her. The first chance I got was as she was leaving a store at the mall." Lorrie had heard enough. She walked into the room and stepped in front of Eric.

"How can you be so unaffectionate," said Lorrie. "Don't you have any feeling for a blood relative?"

"Who are you?" asked Eric being surprised by her.

"You can shoot me and try to kill me," said Lorrie, "and you don't even recognize me."

"You look like Aunt Lorrie," said Eric, "but you can't be her. She is dead. I shot her."

"Well I survived as you can see," answered Lorrie.

"I'm so glad that you survived," said Eric. "After I shot you I began feeling sorry that I did it. You will never believe it, but I am glad that you are alive."

"Well Mark," said the Captain. "Do you have all that recorded?" "I do, but I don't think I will need it," said Mark. "I believe that he is really sorry." Then turning to Eric he reached out and grabbed him by the arm. "Come with me. I am charging you with attempted murder. If you will confess to the judge he will give you a light sentence." As they were walking out the door, Lorrie called out to Eric.

"Eric," she said. "I want you to know that, even though I may not forgive you, I want you to know that I will do all that I can for your mother. I will pay for her surgery"

"God Bless You,"said Eric as he walked out the door. Robert then took Lorrie home. There she took out a dinner she had cooked earlier. There was enough there for the two of them. Lorrie heated it and they both had nice diner.

From that day on Robert and Lorrie continued with the lives they had before Eric's attempt on killing Lorrie. They did everything the same. Lorrie went back to work and Robert went back to writing his novel. The only difference was that they spent a lot of time planning their wedding. About three week later, Captain Wilson called Robert.

"Hello Robert," said the Captain. "How are you doing?"

"I'm fine," said Robert, "and I will not accept a new assignment." "Very funny," said the Captain. "The reason I called is to let you know that Eric is going before Judge Warren tomorrow morning at ten. I think you should be there."

"I'll be there," said Robert. That night Robert told it to Lorrie. He asked whether she wanted to come. She declined.

The next morning at ten Robert was at the courtroom.

"Please stand," said one of the court attendants, "the judge is entering." The judge walked in and sat at his bench.

"I understand that you Eric James are accused of attempted murder," said the judge. "How do you plea?"

"I plead guilty," said Eric.

"Why did you do it," asked the judge, "and do you reepent?" "You honor," said Eric, "It was the dumbest reason. My mother is very ill and needs surgery badly. We do not have the money or insurance for the care she needs. I came here to ask Aunt Loretta for help, but when I learned that she was going to get married I lost my mind. I figured that if she got married he would inherit everything she had. In my confused mind I tried to kill her so that I could inherent some money to pay for my mother's needs. It was the dumbest thing I have ever done."

"Do you really repent doing it?" asked the judge doubting his comments.

"I did not know Aunt Loretta," said Eric. "I had never met her. When I met her at the police station I found her to be the nicest person I ever met. She was not angry with me and just wanted to know why I did it. After I told her it was because of my mother's illness she promised to help her. I talked with my mother yesterday and she told me that Aunt Lorrie was taking care of everything. I love her. How can I not feel sorry for what I tried to do?"

"That sounds like a good reason," said the judge. "How do I know that you will not try something like that again?"

"I was visited by a church pastor several times while I was in jail. He was sent by my Aunt Lorrie. To make the story short he convince be to become a Christian. Yesterday I accepted Jesus Christ as my savior.

I am now a Born-Again-Christian. I will have faith in the Lord from that day on."

"I believe you," said the judge. "Does anyone have anything to add to this hearing," asked the judge.

"I would like to add something," said Robert. "I was with them when Loretta met Eric. I was the one who brought him to his cell. I believe he was truly sorry for what he did. After Lorrie told him that she would take care of his mother he got tears in his eyes. He was crying all the way to the cell. I could tell it wasn't an act."

"Well I accept your plea," said the judge. "Therefore I sentence you to ten years in the state penitentiary." That finished the hearing. They all left and went home. That evening Robert called Lorrie.

"Hi honey," said Robert. "How are you doing?"

"I'm doing fine," said Lorrie. "Why are you calling? This is Tuesday and we don't go out on Tuesday remember"

"I just thought that you wanted to know the outcome of the courtroom hearing," said Robert surprised at her comment.

"That's right," said Lorrie. "I forgot all about that. By the way, I got the invitation cards and am in the process of addressing them."

"Anyway," said Robert. "the hearing is over and Eric was sentenced to ten years in jail."

"I guess he got off pretty leniently," said Lorrie.

"I also found out that you are helping out his mother,: said Robert. "That was very sweet of you."

"After all she was my cousin," said Lorrie. "I didn't do it only for Eric. She is family even though I don't remember her."

"I still think you are very sweet," said Robert. "Have a great evening."

The days rolled by. Robert and Lorrie went back to their normal activities. Finally it was September. All the invitations had been mailed. They heard back from most of them. They were all set for the wedding. It was on the Friday before the wedding they met for the wedding rehearsal that Robert had a strange feeling. He felt like it was all a wonderful dream. He went into a trance. He hardly remembered the rehearsal dinner. He only remembered that his dad gave a toast. Robert didn't remember what he said. The next day was the same. He only remembered Lorrie coming down the aisle. He remembered how beautiful she looked. He felt that he had never seen anything that beautiful before. He remembered kissing her in front of a large audience. The only other thing he remembered was the pastor saying that they were husband and wife. It was on the way to their honeymoon at the Niagara Falls that he came out of his trance. He looked at the person sitting beside him. She was so beautiful. He looked at her hand. It did have the wedding ring on. He looked at his hand. He also had a wedding ring. He suddenly realized that it wasn't a dream. He realized that the wedding had taken place, and the wonderful time he experience last night was not a dream. He then reached out and grabbed Lorrie's hand.

"Lorrie," he said, "do you have any idea on how very much I love you. It is hard to believe that we are married, and on our way to our honeymoon."

"You can't be happier than I am," said Lorrie. "My most wonderful and fantastic dream has cometrue." Robert squeezed her hand. They were on their way to their honey moon. Robert had no idea on how extremely happy they were going to be from that day on.

The end